I REFUSE TO PLAY POWER GAMES WITH YOU," Chelsea said, moving away from him.

"This isn't a game anymore, Chelsea," Craig said, taking a step closer.

She kept edging backward and he kept coming toward her and didn't stop, even when her back touched the wall of the pantry. She felt his heat and strength as he aligned his body to the soft curves of hers. He lifted his hand to her cheek, then brushed his thumb across the fullness of her lower lip.

"You want me. Why don't you admit it?" he demanded, pulling her closer.

"No," she cried, flattening her hands on his chest to push him away. Instead, unable to stop herself, she sank her fingers into the coarse silk that covered his chest and nearly moaned from the pleasure of touching him. . . .

WHAT ARE *LOVESWEPT* ROMANCES?

They are stories of true romance and touching emotion. We believe those two very important ingredients are constants in our highly sensual and very believable stories in the LOVESWEPT *line. Our goal is to give you, the reader, stories of consistently high quality that may sometimes make you laugh, sometimes make you cry, but are always fresh and creative and contain many delightful surprises within their pages.*

Most romance fans read an enormous number of books. Those they truly love, they keep. Others may be traded with friends and soon forgotten. We hope that each LOVESWEPT *romance will be a treasure—a "keeper." We will always try to publish*

LOVE STORIES YOU'LL NEVER FORGET
BY AUTHORS YOU'LL ALWAYS REMEMBER

The Editors

WILDER'S WOMAN

LAURA TAYLOR

BANTAM BOOKS

NEW YORK · TORONTO · LONDON · SYDNEY · AUCKLAND

WILDER'S WOMAN
A Bantam Book / November 1993

If you would be interested in receiving protective vinyl covers for your Loveswept books, please write to this address for information:

Loveswept
Bantam Books
P.O. Box 985
Hicksville, NY 11802

ISBN 0-553-44347-x

Published simultaneously in the United States and Canada

With love to my brothers
Brett, Craig, and Eric

ONE

Chelsea Lockridge tightened her grip on the rung of the heavy metal gate and shoved with all her strength. She managed to move it forward a few more inches. Widening her stance, she pushed again. Rain spattered her face and soaked her dark hair which she'd arranged into a snug chignon that morning before she'd left San Francisco.

Her foot slipped into an ankle-deep puddle, but she held on to the gate and kept herself from falling. Exasperated, she mourned the damage being done to the Italian leather of her low-heeled shoes, her stockings, and the cuffs of her wool slacks, but didn't stop her struggle with the gate. What a time for her first visit to this property! Thunder rumbled and boomed overhead and lightning occasionally split the dark clouds with laserlike flashes, but it was the rain making the iron slippery that was giving her the biggest problem. She had to get this sagging gate open so she could drive into the acreage and find the cabin on it. Her ex-husband had inherited this land from his grandfather, and she'd been paying the taxes on it for the last six years to keep it from being claimed by the state during Craig's absence, but she'd never intended to visit it—until last night.

Several minutes of fruitless effort passed. Chelsea paused to rest, slumping against the gate. As she caught her breath, she cursed her small stature. She was so tired. At first she tried to blame it on the bad day and night she'd had. And she *was* emotionally drained from reading her father's journal and physically under par from a sleepless night. Still, she had to be honest with herself and admit this was one of those times when nature felt compelled to demonstrate to her in spades the limitation of her size.

Frowning, she lifted her head when she heard an unfamiliar sound. Glancing over her shoulder, she saw nothing but the narrow black ribbon of rain-slick pavement she'd traveled earlier and the dense stands of pine that towered on either side of the road. The sound intensified. She identified it then as a motor, and it was coming from the area in front of her, not behind. She clung to the recalcitrant gate, looking over it at a rutted trail that disappeared about twenty yards beyond into the trees.

Suddenly a mud-spattered Jeep burst into the clearing like a fireball exploding out of a burning building. Stunned, Chelsea stared at the vehicle as the driver slammed on the brakes, sending up a geyser of muddy rainwater.

Despite the rain and patches of fog, she could see with surprising clarity the rough-looking, long-haired man who vaulted out of the Jeep, a shotgun gripped in his left hand.

She didn't recognize the man who was stomping toward her, but she did recognize the emotion rolling off him: Fury, barely under control. With apparent contempt for the miserable weather, he wore his black slicker unfastened; it snapped angrily against the sides of his long, muscular legs. His stride, aggressive in the extreme, remained steady and sure despite the rutted ground and the mud sucking at his battered boots.

Chelsea's gaze traveled up his body as he drew closer. She unconsciously measured the snug fit of the jeans that encased his powerful thighs and hugged his groin like the palm and fingers of a lover's hand—a lover who appreciated his blatant maleness. Despite the clothed state of his body, she detected a stomach as flat and as hard as a slab of stone, a chest that strained the fabric and buttons of a faded plaid shirt, and broad shoulders that tugged at the seams of the slicker he wore. Exhaling unevenly, she took in the muscles that corded his strong neck and the dark stubble that covered his chin and jaw.

Something deep inside her lurched unexpectedly. She blinked and focused on his lips. Although compressed into a straight white line, they seemed familiar while simultaneously hinting at an erotic nature that was worthy of her exploration.

Chelsea shuddered, astounded to realize that she was responding to his physical prowess on an instinctively sensual level. She couldn't remember the last time she'd responded to a man— any man. Startled and a little embarrassed, she dragged her gaze higher still; he was furious. Shock rippled through her then. The years and experiences he obviously had endured had changed him in ways she sensed went far deeper than his altered appearance. Chelsea stared at him, her hazel eyes wide and her disbelief holding her immobile.

Craig Wilder paused on his side of the gate, and glared at her.

"Get the hell off my property and don't come back."

Her body jerked involuntarily as if physically assaulted by his words, yet her brain quickly dealt with the reality that the yuppie lawyer she'd married so long ago had become some untamed creature who now felt at home in the sparsely populated high country of northern California. The civilized veneer he'd once worn like armor had been scraped clean. Craig Wilder looked exactly like what he'd become—an angry, thirty-six-year-old ex-con who'd gone to ground in the year since his release from federal prison.

He bore no resemblance to the man she'd once welcomed into her heart and body in the name of love, Chelsea realized with dismay. Although his parole officer had cautioned her, she hadn't believed him when he'd insisted she wouldn't recognize her former husband. Now she wished she'd heeded his warning and planned this visit with more care.

"Leave now, Chelsea!" he shouted. "If you stay, I'll make you wish you hadn't."

Her hands fell to her sides. Deeply shaken,

she searched for the right words to say after not seeing him for six years. She searched, too, for courage, amidst the debris of regret and shame that filled her. She finally found it. She understood his anger, even knew that from his perspective it was a justified response to her unannounced arrival, but she also felt sad. Desperately sad, because they'd both been victimized by a man they'd trusted.

She drew in a steadying breath. "I need to speak with you, Craig."

He scowled at her. "There's nothing left to say."

He started to turn away. She lunged forward, slamming her shoulder into the side of the gate as she snaked her arm through the gap she'd struggled to create. She tried to grab his hand, but her fingers simply slid across the arm of his wet slicker. He recoiled as though repelled by her touch.

Chelsea felt tears sting her eyes at his response to her. Withdrawing her arm, she straightened. She ignored the throbbing in her shoulder, and she consciously refused to cower in the face of his rage and distrust. Although nervous about his reaction to what she had to tell him, she also refused to allow him to intimidate her.

"Five minutes, Craig. That's all I need. It's important."

"I don't owe you five seconds."

"But I owe you," she countered firmly, despite the devastating impact of his rejection.

She endured Craig's angry gaze, and she comforted herself with the memory of a time when his eyes had been warmed by passion. But that was the past, she belatedly reminded herself. A past she still mourned as dead, for it could never be reclaimed.

The rain intensified to a heavy downpour. Thunder crashed deafeningly and lightning zig-zagged across the sky in a kaleidoscopic display. She flinched, chilled to the bone by the storm, but she held her ground, her face lifted for Craig's inspection, her expression neutral.

She finally warned, "I'm not leaving until we talk. I can wait in my car until you're ready to hear what I've come to say." She was prepared to wait for a long time. She'd stopped on the drive this morning and told her boss at the child custody division of family court that an emergency situation would keep her out of work for a while.

He swore, the word so coarse that it shocked her. She couldn't recall a time when he'd used such crude language in front of her. He'd always been protective, the ultimate gentleman bent on safeguarding the woman in his life.

Chelsea tilted her chin higher, appearing defiant even though his close scrutiny made her feel intimidated. But she promised herself that she would be strong and remain calm. For his sake, not her own.

"You've changed."

She heard the accusation in his voice. She bristled, but she saw no sense in denying the obvious. She didn't need any reminders that they'd both been through their own personal versions of hell, or that they'd both been forced to change in order to survive. "You're right," she conceded.

She searched his angular features, hoping for a hint that his anger with her might have eased somewhat in the minutes he'd spent studying her, but she found no softening in his demeanor. If anything, he looked angrier. She silently cursed the man responsible for the changes in Craig.

With a calm she didn't feel, Chelsea remarked, "Events change people. I suspect we've both learned that lesson better than most people ever do."

She realized by the expression on his face that he didn't know what to make of her attitude or her behavior, so she waited for him to come to terms with both. Unless he cooperated, she wouldn't be able to tell him what she'd discovered. She didn't intend to send the new evidence through the mail to him or even offer it to the appropriate legal authorities.

She felt certain that Craig needed to feel—deserved to feel—that he was in control of his world again, even if it meant destroying the reputation of a dead man. The information in her father's journal could allow Craig to undo some of the damage done to his life and his career as an assistant federal prosecutor.

She watched him flick a contemptuous glance at her sports car. His expression told Chelsea that he knew who'd given it to her and exactly what it symbolized. It was a wealthy man's gift to his only child, a toy intended as a substitute for emotions never expressed and closeness never attained, despite the child's adoration of the self-absorbed man she called her father.

"That thing's useless out here. You'd never make it to the cabin."

"I'll walk if I have to," Chelsea announced.

She felt Craig's fury, felt it vibrate through the rain, glimpsed it in his cold gaze, his unyielding features, his taut, muscular body. She said nothing. Gripping the shoulder strap of her purse with chilled fingers, Chelsea simply drew on the patience she'd been forced to learn in recent years and waited.

Craig suddenly jerked the gate open. He seized her by the arm and half walked, half dragged her in his wake. Although startled, Chelsea didn't fight him. Neither did she fear him. She felt only regret that he'd been reduced to such a rage-filled existence. He didn't pause until he reached the Jeep, even though she tripped more than once.

Yanking open the door, Craig ordered, "Get in. I'm not going to stand out here in a thunderstorm just to humor you. You'll have your say, you'll leave, and you won't ever come back. Is that clear?"

She nodded, her dignity tattered. "Very clear."

Turning, she stiffly climbed into the Jeep. As she settled atop the ripped leather seat, she stopped worrying about the mud on her shoes and slacks. The interior of the vehicle was already coated with the stuff.

Very cold despite the heat blasting up at her from the floor vents, Chelsea rubbed her palms together. Craig joined her, his well-developed anatomy dwarfing the interior of the vehicle and reminding her once more that he no longer had the sleek, streamlined physique of a marathon runner. Even the bandanna fastened across his forehead to restrain his long hair gave him a lawless and vaguely menacing appearance. Chelsea sensed in that instant that Craig now possessed the ability to survive the meanest city streets or the darkest threats of incarceration.

There were, she'd long ago realized, predatory creatures in prison, and she assumed that Craig had deliberately redesigned his body as a statement of his determination to thwart any attempts at physical or sexual dominance by other inmates. She felt sickened by the thought that he'd had to protect himself from that kind of perverse victimization.

A muscle ticked in his clenched jaw. His hands were white-knuckled as he gripped the steering wheel. She ached inside for him, and she longed to relieve him of the tension that he felt, but she also ached a little for herself, because he refused to spare her even a glance before he jammed the Jeep into gear and slammed his foot against the accelerator pedal.

The vehicle shot forward. Staring straight ahead, Chelsea gripped the edges of her seat during the bone-rattling, teeth-jarring ride that followed. She tensed, her body instinctively preparing itself for disaster as they careened over the winding, potholed trail that passed for a road.

Craig muttered an angry word a few minutes later and slowed the Jeep to a crawl over a narrow wooden bridge that spanned a deep, water-swollen gully. She stared in fascination at the muddy water below and tried to ignore the way the aged planks moaned and groaned beneath them.

Sighing with relief once they were across and back on the trail, she earned a searing look of disdain from Craig before he returned his attention to driving. The prospect of being alone with Craig in the cabin suddenly frightened her. Not because she feared that he might harm her physically, but because of the emotional vulnerability she still felt around him.

She allowed herself a moment of resentment for the destructive power of others, but then she reminded herself that her goal was to right a wrong, whatever the cost to herself. She knew in her heart that she couldn't fix what had happened to their marriage, because she'd already lost Craig's love and trust. He slammed his foot against the brake pedal, and Chelsea grabbed the dashboard with both hands. The vehicle slid forward several feet and came to a shuddering halt in front of a small, rustic-looking cabin of indeterminate age.

Craig stalked into the cabin without a word or a backward glance. She followed him, then felt the press of his gaze as she stepped inside. Wrapping her arms around her waist, Chelsea looked around at the Spartan interior. The logs burning in the fireplace immediately drew her attention. She crossed the long, rectangular room, noting as she walked the simple furnishings and curtainless windows.

He'd exchanged one cell for another, she realized sadly. She wanted to weep for him, but she sensed that she would provoke her ex-husband if she lost control of her emotions. Chelsea sank down onto the raised outer edge of the hearth, as much to take advantage of the warmth emanating from the fire as to put some distance between herself and Craig, who straightened and eyed her suspiciously after propping his shotgun against the wall by the door.

He paused in the center of the cabin, glowering at her as he shrugged free of his slicker. The sodden garment landed in a heap on the floor. Under Chelsea's watchful gaze, Craig kicked it aside. She lifted her surprise-filled eyes to his face, aware that her response to his disregard for his clothing showed in her face.

A typical yuppie, he'd had a fondness for expensive clothing. She remembered how much his appearance had mattered to him, just as she recalled how he'd prided himself on being meticulously groomed, especially when he was in a courtroom or being interviewed by the media. Gone now was his charismatic personality. Gone as well was the sophisticated image he'd presented to the world. She doubted that his dedication to the public welfare and his desire for a future in the political arena had survived prison, either.

Chelsea didn't recognize or understand this Craig Wilder. He vibrated with hostility, like a wary, wild creature of the forest whose territory had been invaded. His brawny physique, the rigid set of his broad shoulders, and his hard gaze underscored his obvious distrust of her motives. Staring at him, she fought the emotion clogging her throat and blinked back the tears that pooled in her eyes.

His silence wore on her nerves, but she brought herself under control and admitted, "I contacted the parole board. They gave me the name of your parole officer. He told me you were living out here. He said I shouldn't bother you."

"You should have listened to him. He knows how I feel about you."

"He called you, didn't he?"

"Does it matter?"

She exhaled, the sound a reflection of her unease. "Probably not, although you do need to hear what I have to say."

His expression enigmatic, he watched her for several minutes before he spoke. "Save your apologies, Chelsea. I don't want anything from you, especially phony sentiments you'll forget as soon as you utter the words. You were a treacherous bitch when I needed you six years ago, so I'm really very grateful that our life together is a part of the past. I've forgotten it, and I suggest you do the same."

His voice scraped across her emotions like a serrated blade. She shot to her feet, color flooding her cheeks. "I haven't done anything wrong, so I'm not offering you an apology. And I didn't come here to talk about our marriage, because I know it's over. You made your feelings very clear when you divorced me. I also don't expect anything to change between us." Chelsea squared her shoulders. "What I do expect is civility. I'm not the enemy, and you aren't the only one who was harmed by what happened six years ago."

Craig stabbed her with a killing glance and then began to prowl the interior of the cabin.

Chelsea kept a close eye on him as he paced the length and width of the uncarpeted room. He reminded her of an animal fighting the memory of having been caged.

He finally approached her. She sidestepped him, then instantly regretted acting in such a skittish manner. She felt a moment's relief when Craig ignored her, reached for a heavy log from an old metal tub situated on the opposite side of the hearth, and added it to those in the fireplace.

Her eyes stayed fastened on him as he straightened and gazed at the fire. She registered the angular line of his profile and the fact that his jaws were clamped together. When he lifted his chin, she watched his long, bluntly cut hair shift back over his shoulders. It was then that she noticed the small square chunk of gold that he wore in the lobe of his right ear.

Chelsea stopped breathing, mesmerized by his closeness and shocked that he'd had his ear pierced. Holding perfectly still, she waited for Craig to step away so that she could return to the warmth of the fire. He didn't. Instead, he turned and peered down at her, his expression so jaded and suspicious that she couldn't think of anything to say. She'd never felt smaller or more vulnerable. Her heart raced beneath her ribs, and she trembled as her own inner apprehension raced up her spine and raised chill bumps across her nape. But she still couldn't drag her eyes from him. She felt transfixed by the unyielding contours of his features, the pulse throbbing in his temple, and the cynicism that marred the shape of his lips.

She couldn't help wondering what it would be like to touch him now, to feel the differences in his body with her fingertips, to experience once again his passionate nature, even though she sensed the extent of the risk to her emotions if she fell victim to such an impulse. Despite his hard exterior, Craig looked earthy, sensual, rugged, and untamed. He also looked very unpredictable. Her sexual instincts, dormant since his incarceration, called out. She still wanted him.

Don't touch me! she nearly screamed when she saw the unexpected glitter of raw sexual awareness flare in the depths of his eyes. *Oh, God, don't even think of using me, because I'd die if you dishonored the memory of what we once felt for each other.*

TWO

Craig resented the hunger that surged through his veins and hardened his body as he studied Chelsea. He wanted her, craved her with every cell in his body, but he knew better than to indulge his desire. He felt certain that one taste of her, no matter how brief, contained the potential of sending him reeling back into a whirlpool of black emotion from which there would be no escape.

Towering over her, he scoured her features with a relentless gaze as he battled his need to discover if she still possessed the passion and tenderness he'd once found in her arms. Craig cursed his own curiosity a heartbeat later. She'd obviously changed, but no matter how assertive she'd become and no matter how much he wanted her, he reminded himself that she lacked the integrity he now required in a woman.

"I don't like what you've done to your hair," he finally said, although he wondered why it even mattered to him.

Chelsea blinked, but she didn't look away. Lifting her right hand, she fingered the chignon at her nape.

His palms and fingers suddenly tingled with the memory of what it had felt like to touch the waist-length cascade of thick, dark auburn curls when they made love. Her hair always reminded him of the densest silk, and he'd spent long hours playing with it.

Desire lanced through him like a bolt of lightning, a secondary chorus to the chaos taking place outside as it penetrated the control he invariably exercised. He used the gnawing feeling to remind himself he couldn't risk revealing his need to her. Need made a man vulnerable. He'd learned that particular fact of life well before his stint in prison, but the concept had taken on greater clarity during his stay there.

Craig clamped down on the desire stirring in his loins and pummeling his senses. His expression grew even more ruthless, but he ignored the startled look in Chelsea's eyes as she watched him, just as he dismissed his awareness of the tremor of unease that rippled through her slender body. She made him think of a doe on the verge of bolting, but unlike the doe, an essentially innocent creature, Chelsea Lockridge possessed the most duplicitous nature of any female he'd ever known.

"Unpin it."

She blanched. "Craig . . ."

He ordered, "Do it. Now."

Craig watched her, no hint of mercy on his face. His eyes narrowed while she fumbled with shaking fingers to remove the hairpins that anchored the chignon in place. She tucked the pins into the outside pocket of her shoulder bag and shook her hair loose in a gesture so innately sensual that he closed his hands into tight fists to keep from touching her.

He moved closer when she lowered her hands to her sides, his senses alert to the erratic sound of her breathing. He saw fear in her eyes. He knew he'd caused it, and he told himself that he didn't care. Terror had been *his* constant companion for too many years. It was her turn, he concluded, to feel the full force of it. He reminded himself, too, that she deserved any retribution he devised, because she'd abandoned him when he'd needed her most.

Craig raised his hands and drove his fingers

into the dense fall of curls that grazed her shoulders. She flinched beneath his touch, but he caged her head between his hands and held her still. Kneading her scalp, his senses registered the warmth that seeped into his callused skin and the silky strands that curled around his fingers. His hands shook, and his body tightened with an inner tension too long unappeased. Cursing the new onslaught of desire that flowed hotly through his veins, his hold on her tightened. Although he chastised himself for touching her in the first place, he blamed her for tempting him even as he inhaled her fragrance, the same seductive fragrance that had haunted his days and turned his nights into a living hell while trapped in his solitary cell.

He brought her closer, his narrow hips brushing against her lower abdomen as she stared up at him, wide-eyed and barely able to breathe. He deliberately used his hardening body to tell her that he could take her, would take her, if he decided to, and then he changed tactics on her without warning.

Spreading his fingers, he speared them into the depths of the curly, shoulder-length strands, watching her wince when they caught and snagged in a clump of curls. She bit her lower lip, and tears pooled in her thickly lashed eyes. He gave her credit for endurance when she didn't try to pull free of him, but instead tolerated his displeasure with her and his rough handling with a quiet dignity that baffled him at first and then provoked a flash of grudging respect.

"You've never touched me in anger before," she whispered a few seconds later.

He froze, his attention captured by her gaze. Bottomless pools of hazel, her eyes were a revelation. He saw all manner of emotions that he didn't really want to see. With this view came a flood of memories, sensual memories almost too excruciating to recall because of the sense of loss that accompanied them.

Craig knew in his gut that she was remembering too—remembering what it had felt like when he'd had his hands on her naked body, rousing her senses to fever pitch, seducing her heart and soul, tantalizing her emotions, before he brought her to fruition over and over again. Response shuddered through him as he recalled the glorious feeling of sinking into her body, slowly being claimed by her even as he claimed her as his own.

He felt her tremble, saw her eyes flutter closed. He wondered absently if she felt compelled to hide from him. He refused to allow her that luxury. His fingers tightened and then twisted. Chelsea sucked in a ragged breath.

He slid his hands free of her thick hair, down her slender neck, and then curved them over her shoulders. His fingers spasmed, digging into her. She trembled, but didn't make a sound. Then, slowly, she opened her eyes. Anger flooded his mind and senses because he couldn't stop wanting her. Additional fury steamed through his veins because she seemed determined to play the innocent.

"Have you forgotten that my skin bruises very easily?" she asked.

He heard an inner voice of shame call out to him. Reluctantly, he eased his grip on her. "I haven't forgotten anything, Chelsea."

"Neither have I, but hurting me won't change what happened to us."

Although ruddy color stained his high cheekbones, he didn't bother with an apology. He already knew that the more civilized elements of his nature had died a quick death in prison, and he didn't expect a sudden reincarnation. She shouldn't either, he decided.

"You cut it," he accused.

She clearly understood what he meant. "Yes."

Chelsea turned her head, looking beyond

him. Craig winced as her silky hair trailed over the top of his hands. "Why?"

"I'm busy. It's too much work now." She squared her shoulders as she brought her gaze back to his face. "Hurting each other with careless words won't accomplish anything, either."

"How do you know that?"

"It's not in you to treat a woman cruelly."

"You don't know me any longer. Consider yourself fortunate."

"I do know you," she insisted. "I'm strong enough now to bear your anger, Craig, if that's what it takes to get you to listen to me."

His expression turned to stone, and his eyes flashed a clear warning that he was capable of making her pay for every transgression, real or imagined, that she'd ever committed against him. Craig muttered a foul word, the same word he'd used earlier. This time, though, he noticed that Chelsea seemed unfazed by his crude language.

"How do you know anything about me or my anger?"

She shrugged, looking far more calm than he wanted to feel. "I asked. Your parole officer answered most of my questions."

Feeling betrayed yet again, he jerked free

of her and resumed his restless pacing, aware that she reclaimed her seat on the edge of the hearth and simply watched him. Several minutes passed, minutes filled with the sound of his footsteps and the rain as it battered the rooftop of the cabin.

"Will you listen to me now?"

He kept walking, conscious that he'd adopted the habit of pacing during his first months in prison in order to cope with the claustrophobia he suffered when confined for long hours in his windowless, shoe box-shaped cell. "Why should I?"

"You brought me this far, and I don't think it was because you thought I was in danger of melting if I got rained on." She paused, then added in a wistful-sounding voice, "I've been rained on before, Craig."

He stopped abruptly, his hands fisting at his sides. He didn't need to see her face to know that she was remembering an incident from their honeymoon. What was left of his heart twisted painfully in his chest.

They'd been so eager for each other that they hadn't been able to wait until they returned to the privacy of their hotel room in the Napa Valley. They'd found a deserted glade on a back road not far from a well-known vineyard, hurriedly parked their car and spread a blanket in the waist-high grass. They'd satisfied their mutual hunger with an explosive joining of bodies and hearts in spite of the summer rainstorm that had engulfed them within moments of shedding their clothes.

Craig moved forward with the predatory instincts of a man who'd taken every lesson available in the art of survival. "Talk, Chelsea, and then get the hell out of here."

She gripped the straps of her purse, which rested beside her on the hearth. "My father lied when he testified against you."

"Tell me something I don't already know."

"He manufactured the evidence that got you indicted."

Craig paused, the muscles in his body rippling with tension at the mention of his ex-father-in-law. "Old news. Let's go. I'll take you back to your car."

"Dad . . ." She swallowed convulsively. "He framed you for a crime he committed himself, Craig. I found his journal. He confessed to what he'd done before he died last winter. I have it with me."

He recalled that no one had believed him when he'd voiced his suspicion that someone had set him up. Not his attorney. Not the jury.

Not even his own wife. "You're six years too late, so just forget it."

"It's not too late!" she cried as she jumped to her feet. "You can have your conviction over- turned. I'll . . ."

"You'll what?" he ground out, pinning her in place with a hard look. He watched her stum- ble to a stop halfway between the fireplace and his position in the center of the cabin. "What'll you do this time, Chelsea?" he taunted. "Believe in me? Support me? Or will you defend me the way you did before?"

"I'll help you," she promised. "You deserve to have your life back the way it was."

"Right." Craig laughed, the sound short, hard as nails, and totally lacking any real humor.

Chelsea sighed. "I don't understand your attitude. This could change everything for you. People will finally believe that you didn't tam- per with that jury."

"Do you honestly think that my life will ever be the same, or that *I'll* ever be the same? Are you really still so innocent? I wish to God that son of Satan had taught you to see the world the way it really is and not the way you want it to be. Grow up, Chelsea. It's past time. You're thirty years old, so act like it. You can't be Daddy's little girl for the rest of your life."

She took a step forward, then another. "My father is dead, and I was never his little girl! I was an inconvenience to him after my mother died. I was ignored when I was away at school. I was his hostess when he needed one after I graduated from college—but only after he assured himself that I wouldn't embarrass him in front of his political cronies." She took a steadying breath. "My father isn't even the issue right now, except perhaps as a means to an end. You're the issue, Craig. You deserve to practice law again. You'd be able to if we can get your conviction overturned. After we deal with the legal process, I'm sure the bar association would give you a hearing. You'd be reinstated once we prove the truth."

He concealed the shock he felt. She'd changed in more ways than he'd originally grasped, but he still couldn't forgive her betrayal and abandonment. He doubted he ever would.

"And then I can live happily ever after," he said sarcastically. "Going back into court won't accomplish anything now, so why don't you return to your fantasy world and leave me the hell alone?"

"Craig . . ."

"What?" he shouted, anger rising again.

"Give me a chance to help you, please. I

don't care how difficult the job is or how long it takes. I'm willing to work with you every step of the way. What better use is there for the money my father left me than to hire the best legal talent available for your case?"

He lifted his hand, pulled off the bandanna and let it drop to the floor, and massaged his forehead with his fingertips. The pain throbbing in his temples came from the frustration of rehashing a past he couldn't change. He needed to shut out the world. He needed to rid himself of the crazy urge to escape by burying himself in the depths of Chelsea's body for a few short hours. He failed. If anything, he felt less in control than ever.

He knew only one thing: He had to get Chelsea out of the cabin and off his property. For both their sakes, she needed to stay as far away from him as possible. He finally looked at her. "I don't want you here."

"What my father did to you, and to us, was wrong."

"A lot of things are wrong. Starting with you."

She reached out to him with both hands. She reminded him of a supplicant at an altar. He had no intention of forgiving her for the sins she'd committed against him, and he sure as hell wasn't willing to offer her the penance she seemed to be seeking.

Craig gave her a derisive look, shoved past her, and walked to the fireplace. He stood with his back to her, still sorely tempted to take anything she might offer in the way of comfort. He already knew he couldn't have his life back, just as he already understood the futility of nursing the hope that he might get justice.

Justice had failed him during his years in prison, despite one appeal after another. Having existed within the confines of hell for so many years, he believed in one simple concept: Survival.

"I want to help you," she said as she slowly made her way across the cabin.

Craig stared at the fire, his elbow resting against the mantel edge, both his fists clenched as he spoke. "My reputation and my career are gone, and no one can give them back to me, Chelsea. No one."

"What about the future?"

"What future?" he demanded, his voice like a cracking whip. "I don't have one, thanks to you and your father."

"You have every right to hate us," she conceded.

He nearly choked on the need for revenge.

"You owe me. One way or another, you'll pay," he vowed.

"Whether or not you believe it, I have paid. I'm still paying, Craig." She exhaled softly, the sound like a pain-filled caress. "Please don't let your hate and resentment keep you from looking at the new evidence."

He didn't bother to turn around, although the sound of her voice and the scent of her skin warned him that she was close, very close. He tried to keep his feelings concealed, but in the process of not revealing his hunger for her, his bitterness slipped past the barriers he'd constructed around his emotions. "You should have cared enough to help me when it would have counted for something. You're too late."

She placed her hand on his shoulder, her fingers curving gently over the worn fabric that covered his warm skin. He felt her touch right down to his shattered soul.

"I just discovered the truth yesterday afternoon. I was cleaning out his office, boxing books and case files that he'd donated to his law school library. Craig, his confession could change your life. If I'd known about it any sooner, I would have moved heaven and earth to help you. I swear it."

He shrugged free of her hand, still fighting

his memories of her sensuality and the urge he felt to possess her as he turned on her. "You should have *known* I was innocent."

"I've always believed in your innocence, but . . . but there were things happening back then, things I never had a chance to tell you," she finished in a whisper.

Renewed anger burst to life inside of him, adding fuel to his determination to get her out of his life once and for all. "Go to hell," he said in a low, lethal tone of voice, "and take your so-called evidence with you."

He watched her shoulders slump before she turned away from him. "I'll leave the journal." She made her way across the room. "Read it when you're ready. If you want my help, you have it. I'll do anything you ask of me."

Forcing himself not to move, he counted her footsteps to keep himself from grabbing her and carrying her off to his bed. His eyes blazed in his hard-featured face as she paused beside a small wood table and tugged a bulky leather volume out of her shoulder bag.

She smoothed her shaking fingertips over the spine of the book, placed it on the table, and went to the door. Without looking back, she said, "I didn't have time to make a copy, so be careful with it."

Craig surged forward, moving with the silence and speed of a striking puma. Slamming his open palm against the center of the door as Chelsea turned the doorknob, he met her startled gaze with a coldly speculative expression.

"Anything?" he asked in a low, grit-filled voice, the need that vibrated through his body making him reckless.

Chelsea gave him a puzzled look. She opened her mouth to speak, but snapped it shut a moment later. Her eyes widening with dawning comprehension, she simply stared up at him while all the color drained from her cheeks.

"Anything, Chelsea?" Craig prodded, forcing himself to ignore her shocked expression.

She stiffened. "I'm not a whore, so don't treat me like one. If you need a woman to relieve an ache, then find one who's willing to be used."

"Chelsea . . ." His voice held a note of warning, but he heard something more, something he didn't want to believe, something he feared she might have heard too.

A tear slipped down Chelsea's cheek. He stared in fascination, not simply in disbelief that she'd allowed him to witness the hurt he'd inflicted.

"Take care of yourself," she urged, speaking so softly that he strained to hear her. "I'm sorry my father was such a selfish man."

Craig frowned, baffled by her behavior. He slowly stepped aside, his gaze growing more troubled as he watched her pull open the door and step out onto the shallow front porch. She didn't look back, even though he stood in the open doorway as she ran from him.

Chelsea quickly disappeared into the embrace of the fog and heavy rain that blanketed the surrounding landscape. Left alone, Craig struggled to come to terms with the fact that he'd nearly pleaded with her to remain with him.

THREE

Heedless of the storm, Chelsea dashed out of the cabin and across the clearing. Instinct, not simply the compelling urge to escape Craig's contempt, anger, and pain guided her onto the trail.

She hugged her shoulder bag to her chest as she ran, her emotions shattered, her thoughts so fragmented that she couldn't focus on anything but her need to be alone and nurse her wounds in private. Time, the great healer, wouldn't banish her anguish, though. She knew that deeply.

Slipping and stumbling, she made her way along the rutted trail. She managed to keep moving by sheer force of will.

The simple, awful truth was that she still

loved Craig, despite the years they'd spent apart, the divorce he'd initiated, or how much prison had changed him. She would always love him. And she owed him. No one else had the power to make amends for the injustice inflicted upon him by her father.

Her footsteps slowed as she approached the bridge that spanned the ravine. Shivering with cold, Chelsea paused and studied the sagging expanse of old timbers. Thunder boomed menacingly overhead. Lightning crackled and hissed, and she jumped in surprise when a huge tree limb fell to the ground only a few feet from where she stood.

Chelsea trembled, as much from the cold as the unknown. A city girl, she felt insignificant as she glanced around. She found the absence of buildings and people unnerving. How could Craig cope with such isolation?

Buffetted by the heavy wind, the pine trees all around her swayed and creaked. She warily observed the leaves and twigs that danced atop wind gusts, while squat shrubs clung to the earth with the kind of tenacity Chelsea normally credited to human beings who reached deep within themselves for an extra measure of strength when challenged by a crisis.

Aware that she had no other option, she

set aside her apprehension and stepped onto the bridge. She froze a moment later when something crashed against one of the pilings that supported the structure. Once the bridge stopped shivering beneath the impact of the heavy object, she took another step. The timbers beneath her feet moaned ominously.

She exhaled shakily, but she remained resolute in her determination to get to her car. More frightened than she'd been in years, she tried with only marginal success to convince herself that she didn't weigh enough to threaten the stability of the bridge. When she heard an odd squealing sound, it reminded her of a child crying out in distress.

Fear nearly choking her, Chelsea suddenly realized that the sound could have come from a wild animal. She glanced over her shoulder, but she saw nothing more threatening than the windswept trail. Whispering a prayer, she peered at the current of muddy water charging recklessly down the ravine. She consciously squared her shoulders, gathered her courage, and forced aside her awareness of the now constant moaning and shimmying of the timbers beneath her feet.

Cautiously inching forward, Chelsea heard a sudden, deafening roar and paused in midstride.

She stared in horror as a wall of water exploded into the ravine, then told herself to run before it slammed into the bridge. She did, but the water moved with terrifying speed. The rotting timbers under her pitched, then buckled as they were subjected to the punishing pressure of the water.

Casting aside her purse, Chelsea struggled for balance as the center of the bridge began to break apart and drop into the ravine. Falling to her knees, she groped for a hold in the same instant that the torrent flowed over the age-weakened structure and slammed into her like a heavy fist. Her scream died as she was pitched into the air and tossed like a discarded rag doll into the vicious current.

Tumbling head over heels, Chelsea was jabbed by pieces of wood. Suddenly she was caught in a deadly underwater swirl. Submerged, she continued to struggle despite her fear that she was on the verge of drowning. She held her breath, and her lungs burned for want of oxygen. She could barely reason, but out of the chaos came an unexpected reprieve. A sharp curve in the ravine provided a natural safety net for her body.

Plastered against the side wall of the ravine by the strength of the current just seconds later,

Chelsea lifted her face out of the water and gasped for air. She finally caught her breath, shoved her long hair out of her face with her free hand, and opened her eyes. Stunned by the dunking she'd just endured, she belatedly registered the tree limb that held her in place between the steep face of the ravine and a large boulder that jutted out of the water.

Despite her panic, Chelsea concentrated on not being pulled back into the whirling current. Turning, she peered upward, her teeth chattering from the cold. The ravine was steep and she saw little that would help her climb to safety. There were a few chunks of rock on the slope and the exposed roots of a tree, but nothing more promising in the way of hand or footholds.

Tears of frustration filled her eyes, blurring her vision, but she blinked them back. Clinging to the boulder, she conserved her strength, resting for a few moments before she attempted to scale the ravine. Fatigue and cold gripped her body. She tightened her hold on the boulder, and while the current surged and sucked and thrashed around her, she permitted herself the small luxury of recalling the time in her life when Craig Wilder had still loved her. Although tempted to linger in her memories, she found unexpected strength in them and used them to motivate herself.

Summoning her courage, she reached up and closed one hand around a clump of tree roots. She simultaneously shifted her body so that she could use the boulder for leverage and managed to get her other hand on the roots too. Chelsea paused and gasped for breath, then pulled herself halfway out of the water. The muscles in her slender arms burned as they bore the weight of her suspended body.

After Craig watched Chelsea disappear into the fog, he lost track of time as he stood in the doorway of the cabin, his thoughts on the past, his gaze blank, and his emotions in turmoil. Thunder clapped violently overhead. Lightning split the trunk of a tree in the center of the small clearing in front of him. It toppled over a moment later and crashed to the ground, but he didn't even flinch.

Craig finally felt the cold driven rain. Slamming the door behind him, he paced the interior of the cabin, the heels of his boots striking the wooden floor in a relentless pattern that sounded like nails being pounded into a coffin—

the coffin that held his memories of the life he'd once shared with Chelsea.

Craig paused and looked around the deserted cabin. Chelsea was making her way alone and on foot to the front gate of his property in this vicious storm! In the next moment he remembered the unstable bridge that spanned the ravine about a mile from his cabin.

Craig swore, full of self-loathing. Not bothering with his shotgun or slicker, he ran from the cabin and climbed into the Jeep, his thoughts focused on getting to Chelsea before she reached the old bridge. Her continued presence posed a threat to his emotions, but, Craig knew, the dilapidated expanse of rotting timbers posed an even greater threat— to Chelsea's life.

Tortured by the images of disaster that filled his mind, Craig drove at top speed. The Jeep skidded and fishtailed on the curving, mud-slick trail. He vividly recalled the dangers of flash floods he'd seen as a child on visits with his late grandfather. He felt like a fool for allowing Chelsea to leave the cabin in such a violent storm.

With his emotions in turmoil, he pictured Chelsea being caught on the bridge while a wall of water came barreling down out of the higher elevations. As ferocious as an out-of-control train, a flash flood invariably destroyed everything and everyone in its path.

His self-loathing doubled, because he'd known for a long time how fragile the bridge had become and he hadn't bothered to repair it. Driving across it, in good weather or in bad, had become his way of laughing in the face of the devil. Childish, rebellious behavior, but he'd considered it his right to act recklessly after the regimentation he'd endured during his years in prison.

As Craig observed the intensifying downpour and wind-whipped pines bordering the trail, his facial expression grew grimmer with every passing second. He braked as he rounded the last curve. The Jeep slid to a stop just a few feet from the splintered remains of the bridge.

Stunned by the devastation before him, he jammed the Jeep into park, automatically reached for the coiled rope he kept behind the driver's seat, and sprang out of the vehicle, but he only took a few steps. He shouted Chelsea's name. He repeatedly called out to her, but the only reply he received came from the water raging down the steep ravine.

Craig's gaze fell to the ground. He spotted

Chelsea's abandoned purse, retrieved it, and dug his long, blunt-tipped fingers into the expensive wet leather. He moaned, the sound utterly primal, before he tossed the only evidence of his ex-wife's presence at the bridge onto the hood of the Jeep.

"Please be alive. Please be alive." The words he spoke were the closest thing to a prayer he'd managed in years.

Determined to find Chelsea, Craig crashed through the thick brush that hugged the northern edge of the ravine. Heedless of the tree branches that tore at his clothes and scratched his hands and face, he tracked the downward flow of the water, searching every nook and cranny of the ravine with a piercing gaze and the desperation of a man driven to find his mate—although he fought to reject the latter impulse.

Suddenly Craig heard a cry. He dashed in the direction of the sound. His gaze dropped, and he spotted Chelsea clinging to the side of the ravine. Relief made him weak as he fell to his knees for a better look at her, but the feeling faded when he realized that she was trying to scale the unstable mud bank by using rain-soaked root clumps as handholds.

"Don't move, Chelsea!" he shouted, aware

that he might not be able to save her if she fell backward and was claimed again by the racing current.

Don't move?

She froze, stunned because she thought she'd just heard Craig's voice. Her common sense asserted itself and insisted that she'd imagined the sound. He was still in his cabin. Her mind, she decided, had already started playing tricks on her. She attempted to refocus on the task at hand, in spite of the swirling current that kept trying to drag her back down into the flooded ravine. "If I don't move, I'll die," she told herself.

"Chelsea! Listen to me, dammit!"

She looked up and blinked, the heavy rain obscuring her vision as she dangled half in, half out of the water surging against her lower body. She felt light-headed, and sagged suddenly, her head falling forward. Craig was just a figment of her imagination. As she tried to clear her muddled mind, her fingers cramped, but she marshaled her dwindling strength and maintained her hold on the tree roots.

Above her, Craig looped his rope around a

tree trunk and knotted it securely. He descended the side of the ravine, the rappelling skills he'd acquired in the military many years earlier automatically returning. A cascade of mud clumps and small rocks followed him.

"Chelsea!"

Shocked to hear Craig's voice again, she lifted her head and opened her eyes. "You're real," she said, her disbelief giving way to the almost overpowering urge to reach out and touch him.

"Of course I'm real."

Chelsea watched him frown. She felt the sweep of his dark eyes as they skimmed her features, but she didn't understand what he was looking for. "I thought . . . I imagined you."

His expression hardened. "Pay attention and do exactly what I say."

She nodded, her teeth chattering. He edged close enough to touch. She wanted to crawl into his arms. She wanted him to hold her. And she wanted to hear him say that he'd make everything all right, but the expression on his face convinced her that he wouldn't appreciate her thoughts.

Craig spread his legs and used his feet to brace himself against the side of the ravine as he adjusted his grip on the rope. "I'm going to shift sideways," he shouted above the steady roar of the water. "I want you to wrap your legs around my waist, then put your arms around my neck. We have to move quickly. Do you understand?"

She felt dazed and disoriented, but she grasped his sense of urgency. "Yes."

"I'll get you out of here, Chelsea. Just trust me."

"I do," she insisted, doing her best to remain clearheaded. "I always have." She saw by the look in his eyes that he didn't believe her, but this was not the time or the place to try to persuade him that she spoke the truth. He shifted his body into the position he'd described, and she clumsily followed his instructions when he repeated them.

"Don't let go!" Craig yelled once Chelsea molded herself to him. Using a hand-over-hand method of ascent, he piggybacked her up the steep face of the ravine with a speed and upper body strength that astounded her.

Rolling free of him and onto her back once they reached the ledge above the ravine, she trembled from a combination of relief and shock. Craig quickly pushed himself to his feet. Chelsea welcomed his touch as he pulled her up from the wet ground and then steadied her while she fought the dizziness that seemed determined to drive her back down to her knees.

Grasping her chin, he studied her face. "You look like hell." His gaze narrowed as she peered up at him, her body shaking from the cold, her eyes beginning to glaze with shock. "Let's get out of here. You're inches away from a bad case of hypothermia."

She jerked free of him, stung by his harshness. She took two steps and stumbled, grabbing at a tree trunk, but her knees buckled and she crumpled to the ground. Chelsea heard Craig's disgust with her in the words he muttered before he seized her and swung her up into his arms.

"I can walk. Just give me a chance to catch my breath."

"You've lost your shoes," he reminded her, his tone of voice flat.

She looped her arms around his shoulders and pressed her face against the muscular curve that joined his neck and shoulders. Too drained to fight Craig any longer, Chelsea huddled against his chest as he carried her to the Jeep. She didn't utter a sound. Lulled by the warmth of his hard body, she savored the security she found in his arms.

Craig tucked her into the passenger seat of

the Jeep with competent hands and an impersonal attitude that made her want to cry, but she held herself in check. Chelsea watched him stow her purse and the rope he'd used for his trip into the ravine in the rear of the Jeep, but she looked away from his probing gaze once he climbed into the vehicle.

Easing her head back on the seat, she closed her eyes. She shuddered, the cold so deeply embedded in her bones that she doubted she'd ever get warm again. When Craig's hand settled on her shoulder, she gave him a wary look and he quickly withdrew his hand.

"How do you feel?"

"All right. Just cold. I was so frightened," she admitted.

"Forget what just happened. You've survived the experience, and it's over now." As he spoke, he shifted gears and repositioned the Jeep so that it faced the trail leading back to his cabin.

"I can't believe you actually found me."

"It's a damn good thing I did."

"How did you know I was in trouble? How did you even know where to search?"

He shot her a look she didn't understand. "Does it matter?"

She searched his face, desperate for a glimpse of the old Craig, the compassionate, sensitive man she'd once known so intimately, but she saw nothing to suggest that he existed any longer. "I guess it doesn't," she conceded.

Craig navigated the trail that led back to his cabin in silence and with unusual care, but Chelsea felt every jarring inch they traveled. She suspected that the drive lasted less than two minutes, but it seemed to take hours. She stared straight ahead as they barreled down the trail. Her shivering grew more pronounced, and she bit her lip to keep from begging Craig to stop the Jeep and share his warmth again.

Despite her determination to make her way into the cabin under her own steam, her legs failed to support her as she climbed out of the vehicle. Craig caught her as she fell. She didn't try to stop him as he carried her into the bathroom, held her upright with one hand, then turned on the shower. As he stripped her of her soggy, mud-stained clothing, she could only focus on how disturbingly impersonal his touch was.

He guided her into the shower stall and positioned her beneath the flow of warm water. "Stay put," he ordered so sharply that it immediately set her teeth on edge. "I'll be right back," he said, then jerked the shower curtain closed.

Chelsea slid down the tiled wall, too weak

to remain on her feet. She wrapped her arms around her upraised knees and bowed her head, exhaustion claiming her as the water cascaded across her body. She lost track of time as she sat there, and she welcomed the fatigue-induced lethargy that enveloped her. When she felt strong hands trying to lift her to her feet a little while later, she slapped at them.

"Quit behaving like a child."

She opened her eyes and glared at Craig, her temper flaring for the first time that day. "I'm tired, so leave me the hell alone." She felt him measure her belligerence with a steady, emotionless gaze, and she resented him for being in control. Belatedly recalling her nakedness, she folded her arms across her breasts. "I can take care of myself, Craig. I don't need you."

He chuckled, the sound as dry as rustling paper. "I guess you'll live, but only if we manage to keep you from coming down with pneumonia." He kept his eyes fastened on her face as he removed his boots.

Her dignity in shreds, she closed the curtain and backed up against the tiled shower wall. "I don't want your company, and I don't need your help."

"You don't have a choice." Although still clad in his rain-soaked shirt and jeans, he stepped into the shower. "You're filthy, and this is the only way to get you clean and warm at the same time."

"Get out," she shouted, but he ignored her order.

"How much of that muddy ravine water did you drink?" he asked as he reached up and adjusted the water pressure.

"None. Now please get out of here."

"I've seen you naked before. Would you feel better if I remove my clothes?" He lifted his fingers to the button that secured the waistband of his jeans. "I guess you're curious to see if you can still turn me on," Craig speculated. "Any naked woman would, I imagine, especially after the way I've lived. Enough said?"

"You're being cruel."

"For your sake, I'm being practical," he countered tersely.

Chelsea turned her back on him and pressed her forehead against the shower wall. "Leave me alone," she begged, her voice splintering with emotions she could no longer contain or control.

"I can't, little one. I just can't."

FOUR

Chelsea refused to look at Craig, even when he tugged her out of the corner of the spacious shower stall and turned her around to stand in front of him. She closed her eyes, willing herself not to respond to him, but she sensed the futility of issuing such a command to her dazed senses.

She knew that he cared little about her pride or her modesty when he pulled her arms away from her breasts and forced them down to her sides. She immediately resented his disregard for her emotional state as he lathered her shoulder-length hair with a scented liquid soap, massaging her scalp and nape with strong fingers that provoked memories of the intimacies they'd once shared—memories she'd tried but failed to forget during their years apart.

"I can wash myself," Chelsea insisted.

"You need my help, so don't be stubborn about accepting it." Filling his palms once more with the fragrant soap, Craig moved closer. Instead of a washcloth, he used his large callused hands on her.

Their bodies brushed as he circled her shoulders with his arms and stroked the length of her back with his hands. He left a trail of hot sparks in his wake, and she felt every single one of them. Trembling as Craig leaned over her to reach her hips and the backs of her thighs with his soap-covered hands, Chelsea bit her lip to keep from flinging herself into his arms and begging for a glimpse of the lover she remembered.

"I don't appreciate your behavior at all," she announced shakily, even though she felt like purring.

"When was the last time a man bathed you?"

Her eyes snapped open. Chelsea vibrated with shock and anger. She understood his real question. Had she been with other men during their years apart? She made him wait while she brought herself under control.

"I don't recall," she answered, deliberately lying, because she didn't trust his motives enough to admit the truth, which was that no other man had ever touched her intimately.

Craig straightened, his gaze skimming her face. Chelsea lifted her chin, a clear sign to him of an inner well of defiance that had expanded within her in recent years.

He cupped her shoulders. Chelsea felt the strength in his fingers as he massaged her skin. Sucking in her breath, she savored the sensual glide of his hands as he swept them down her arms. His gaze narrowed and fixed on her face, Craig linked their fingers together in a loose weave that allowed him to massage the hollows between each finger as he studied her.

She felt her anxiety escalate as she experienced the sensual promise of his touch in every nerve. He shifted his thumbs into her palms and rubbed the centers with a suggestive circular motion. Already in danger of blacking out, Chelsea released the air trapped in her lungs in a telling rush.

"Try to remember," he suggested, his voice low and intense.

Craig dragged his knuckles back and forth across her belly, then up and down her midriff, stimulating her senses even more and shattering her soul into a thousand shards of regret over the love lost to them. She came close to weeping in distress. She used her pride to guard her tender emotions and maintain her self-control, but she did give in to his order, reluctantly recalling their past, memories flooding her mind with a vengeance. She remembered Craig's sensual nature, not just his skill as a lover. She even remembered his patience with her lack of experience the first time they'd made love. And she remembered the joy and pleasure she'd felt because he'd been the first person in her life to make her feel truly loved and valued for herself. Their past was a dangerous place to visit, she sternly reminded herself.

Exhaling raggedly, Chelsea reached for his shoulders when he knelt in front of her and smoothed his soapy hands down the length of her legs. He lingered at her feet, his seductive fingers massaging her until she felt nearly mindless. He slid his hands up her legs. When she felt his fingers stroke her inner thighs, she managed not to cry out despite the sensations glittering beneath the surface of her skin. Chelsea shuddered delicately, emotional hunger and physical desire coalescing within her even as she battled her response to his touch.

"Do you remember yet?" Craig asked, surging to his feet to tower over her.

Turning her head, she stared at the tiled

wall beside them. Her insides quickened as he molded the flaring shape of her hips with his hands. He trailed his fingertips up her sides, then reversed course to span her waist. She refused to look at him, even though she hungered for a glimpse, and perhaps even a taste, of his sensual mouth.

She'd spent years dreaming about this, and now she wanted to cry out her need for fulfillment in his arms, but she didn't. Her breasts swelled and firmed, as though begging for the feel of his hands. Chelsea almost pounded on his chest with her fists to vent her frustration, but she managed to quell the impulse.

"Answer me, Chelsea."

"I don't remember much of anything," she finally murmured.

"I know you're feeling pretty beat up right now. You'll be able to rest soon."

She heard unexpected kindness in his voice, and she felt seduced by the sound. She nearly groaned as he trailed his fingertips along the undersides of her breasts, then jerked in surprise when he plucked at her nipples. She couldn't stop the instinct that prompted her to lean closer, especially when he put his hands over the fullness of her breasts.

She closed her eyes on a soft sigh, the utter

rightness of Craig's possessive touch too much to resist. She moaned her need as her nipples tightened into painful little buds of sensation, and when the place at the top of her thighs throbbed and grew humid with need, a whimper slipped past her lips.

"You haven't changed, have you?" he demanded, his voice hard and cold.

Chelsea flinched and opened her eyes, dismay settling over her like a heavy blanket when she saw the harshness in his features. She felt his hands fall away from her breasts, and she accepted the truth. He felt compelled to torture, arouse, and even dominate her with his intimate forays in retribution for the past. She realized, too, that he probably intended to strip her of her dignity, if he could. And, she feared he could.

"You redefine combustibility, Chelsea Lockridge. It's nice to know that some things stay the same."

The matter-of-fact tone of his voice infuriated her, and she demanded, "What exactly are you trying to prove? That you're stronger than I am? That you can arouse my body, even if you can't reach my heart? That you're a man with an agenda that includes humiliating your ex-wife for every mistake she's made in her life? Tell me, Craig, because I'd really like to understand what you're trying to prove."

He shrugged, then used his open palms in a back-and-forth motion to graze the tips of her distended nipples. Chelsea gasped as fire-bursts of sensation exploded deep inside her body.

Craig smiled, his satisfaction with her reaction apparent. "That I was right about you. You've always been like dry kindling just waiting for a lighted match."

She stepped back and consciously reclaimed her pride, her spine stiffening as she peered up at him. "Now that you've proven how easy I am, are you finished punishing me? Or should I look forward to more of the same until I can get out of here?"

She watched his gaze harden, but she felt incapable of compassion or empathy. If anything, she felt detached from reality as she studied his dark eyes—eyes that held all the warmth of cold black granite. She must have imagined that what she'd heard in his voice seconds before was kindness.

Ignoring her questions, Craig completed the task of scrubbing and rinsing her body. He conveyed through his stony expression and steady hands the fact that he would have treated a stranger, or a stack of dishes, with the same emotionless efficiency.

Chelsea seethed with barely suppressed fury while her nerve endings fluttered in distress and her emotions grew increasingly conflicted. Shaken, she escaped his hands and vaulted out of the shower stall.

Craig turned off the water and followed her, his long-legged stride eliminating the space between them in a matter of seconds. Seizing a towel from the stack he kept on a nearby shelf, he grabbed Chelsea's shoulder before she reached the door and spun her around.

Feeling like a cornered animal, she lifted her hand and swung it at Craig, instinct more than common sense driving her. But he caught her wrist before her palm connected with his hard cheek.

"Don't ever try that again," he warned, his voice tight and the muscles in his body rippling with coiled tension.

Chelsea wrenched free of his hold, painfully aware that he permitted her to do so. "I was wrong about you earlier. You are capable of incredible cruelty."

He flinched, then jerked her forward to stand between his powerful thighs. "I warned you, Chelsea, but you obviously didn't listen."

She immediately felt the heat emanating from his hard body. Inhaling sharply, she tried to steady herself as his musky male scent slammed into her senses like a blow. She grappled with the stunning realization that she wanted him with a hunger that transcended her anger. Never having experienced such a shocking rush of pure lust, she glared up at him, her body stiff with disbelief and indignation.

"You're wrong, Craig. I did listen, but you didn't bother to warn me that you'd left your conscience and your morals in prison."

A muscle ticked in his clenched jaw as he circled the bath towel around her wet body like a sarong and then tucked one end into her cleavage to hold it in place. Helpless to stop the trembling that had taken hold of her body, Chelsea held her breath until Craig withdrew his hands.

The expression on his face unreadable and his voice level, he told her, "I survived six years in a sewer of humanity, and I'm capable of things you can't even begin to imagine, so don't push me too hard. You won't like the reaction you get."

Devastated by his attitude and the turmoil within her own heart, she backed away from him until she bumped against the door. Chelsea fumbled with the knob, asking, "Why won't you believe that I came here to help repair the damage my father did to your life?"

Craig remained motionless in the center of the bathroom long after Chelsea left. He concentrated on calming himself by breathing deeply and then exhaling slowly, a skill he'd acquired in prison and not in the courtroom as an assistant federal prosecutor.

Muttering curses at himself, he stripped off his soaked clothing with hands that still shook from the desire raging through him, dried his aroused body with a large bath towel, and shrugged into the terry robe he took from the back of the bathroom door.

He wanted to blame Chelsea for his wild sexual hunger, but his conscience wouldn't let him. She hadn't come on to him. He had deliberately provoked and frightened her. Although he longed to dismiss the guilt he felt as a useless emotion, he couldn't, so he stopped trying.

Moving to the mirror, Craig wiped away a circle of steam and grimaced at the man who stared back at him. The weathered features of that haunted-looking creature revealed the years he'd lost and the price he'd paid for survival. His eyes reflected both his craving for revenge and the cynicism that had corroded his heart. Trying to be honest with himself, Craig silently acknowledged that this was yet another moment when he wanted someone—anyone— to pay for the injustice committed against him. He believed that Chelsea had participated in his downfall, and no matter how much he desired her sexually, he couldn't bring himself to forgive her past actions. He might need her, a need that was purely physical, and he intended to have her, but only on his terms.

Craig pondered her real motives for coming to him as he dumped their wet clothing on the floor of the shower for washing later. No matter what she'd said earlier, he discarded the notion that she intended to drag the reputation of a father she'd idolized through the mud. He knew in his gut that Chelsea wasn't capable of exposing the truth about the bastard who'd destroyed his life.

He left the bathroom, and found Chelsea seated on the edge of the brick hearth. Pausing, he watched her run her fingers through her hair, which suddenly reminded him of a curly auburn cloud now that the heat of the fire had partially dried it. Because she seemed lost in thought as she stared at the fire, Craig allowed himself a leisurely inspection of her. She looked more fragile than usual and far too innocent.

Renewed hunger twisted deep in him. He felt his pulse accelerate. He looked at her bare limbs, then at the tantalizing swell of her breasts. His memories of her vibrantly sensual nature burst across the landscape of his mind in a series of erotic images that he felt helpless to stop.

Remembering the heart-stopping pleasure he'd found in the fragrant hollows and curves of her body, Craig's muscular frame tightened into a series of knots. He hungered in that instant for a taste of her sensitive nipples, while simultaneously recalling the pebble-hard feel of them when he'd made love to her with his lips and tongue. He suppressed a groan and worked at controlling the desire running rampant within him. Although it took him several minutes, Craig finally mastered his impulse to claim Chelsea.

She glanced up at him when he walked toward her. "Why?"

He understood her question, but he hesitated to provide an answer. He didn't trust her enough to be honest about emotions he didn't completely understand himself. He also felt that risking her betrayal twice in one lifetime was far too high a price to pay for a temporary reprieve from the isolation that had become a way of life.

Studying her delicate features, Craig saw disillusionment and hurt reflected in her thickly lashed eyes. While it bothered him more than he wanted to admit, he reminded himself that he couldn't afford to waste his time feeling sorry for her.

"If you hate me so much, why didn't you just let me drown?" As she waited for his reply, she shifted her gaze to the flaming logs.

"I'm a convicted felon on parole, and I don't need the hassle of explaining to the authorities why some idiot woman died of her own stupidity on my property during the worst thunderstorm in the last decade, especially when that woman happens to be my ex-wife."

"I didn't fall into the ravine on purpose!"

"I know exactly what happened."

She trembled. "You couldn't know. You weren't there."

Aware that he'd nearly caused her death, he angrily snapped, "You showed up here without an invitation, so deal with the consequences of the choice you made, and be thankful you're still alive."

Clearly shocked by his lack of empathy, she

stared at him. Craig leaned down, seized her hands, and pulled her to her feet.

"Why do you hate me so much?" she asked. "Why can't you give me a chance?"

"No one gave me a chance!"

"Then at least stop assigning motives to my actions. I didn't come here with a personal agenda, Craig. I came because I . . ." She hesitated, fear flashing in her eyes.

Finally, he thought. The truth. He suspected that she was rattled enough to reveal it. "Why did you really come here, Chelsea?"

"Because it was the right thing to do," she said in a reserved tone of voice.

He shook his head, his frustration with her escalating. "I don't believe you."

Chelsea raised her hands and pressed her fingertips to her temples, loosening the towel that covered her. Craig recognized the troubled gesture for what it was, but he didn't acknowledge his comprehension that her head was throbbing from the stress of the last several hours. Instead, he reached out and grabbed her towel before it parted and exposed her naked body. He slipped his fingers into the valley that separated her breasts with the ease of a man who knew quite intimately the body of the woman who stood before him.

She lowered her hands and eyed him warily. Chelsea started to step backward. His hold on her tightened. Their eyes met and locked, and they both knew she risked losing more than her towel if she moved again.

Breathing shallowly, Chelsea said, "Please don't."

He gripped the fabric even more snugly, his message to her clear as his knuckles pressed against her warm skin. His gaze seared her as it slid over her flushed cheeks, past the pulse throbbing at a hectic pace in the hollow of her throat, and down to the upper swells of her quivering breasts. "Don't what?" he demanded.

"Don't take advantage of me. You never behaved this way when . . ."

" . . . when we were married?" he finished for her as he tore his gaze from her breasts and raised it to her face.

Chelsea nodded warily.

"I don't make promises I don't expect to be able to keep."

"Craig, I won't let you use me."

"You want me," he countered.

She shook her head in denial.

He inhaled sharply, drenching his senses in the fragrance of her soft skin. "Don't lie to me, Chelsea. You're more transparent than glass."

"I don't deserve to be used."

"You and your father used me. Seems like a fair exchange, don't you think?"

"You're an honorable and fair man," she began.

"Get rid of your illusions about me for both our sakes!" he shouted.

She bit her lip and looked away. "I refuse to believe that the man I knew and the years I spent with you were an illusion. I also refuse to believe that you'd use me. We have a history you can't ignore."

"I'm starting to think I've overrated your charms," he cut in, needing to prove to both of them what he believed to be the truth. He had changed. He'd become heartless and soulless, thanks to a dysfunctional penal system, a scheming father-in-law, and a faithless wife.

He studied Chelsea through narrowed eyes, his expression the ultimate in cold sexual speculation and guaranteed to bruise her sense of self-worth. He felt her tremble with shock when he pushed her backward and looked her up and down. "My needs these days are quite . . . basic. Any sexy, soft-skinned woman will do the trick, and you qualify."

She caught the towel before it separated. Although pale, she stood her ground. Fisting her hand in the fabric, she clutched it against her breasts, which seemed on the verge of spilling free if she breathed too deeply. "You'd make love to a woman who isn't willing?"

"Love?" He laughed bitterly. "I'm talking about sex, Chelsea. Pure, hot sex and I guarantee you'd be more than willing pretty damn fast."

"You aren't an animal," she whispered. "Why are you acting like one?"

"I'm not?" he challenged. "My former jailers would probably disagree with you."

"I don't know you at all, do I?"

Craig shrugged, released her without another word, and stepped away from her, but he didn't go far. He paused on the opposite side of the hearth and reached for a log to add to the fire, his profile looking as though it had been carved from stone.

"I think you've built some very high walls around your emotions," she said in a shatteringly gentle tone of voice. "And I suspect you've built those walls to protect what's left of the sensitive and compassionate man I once knew and loved."

Craig froze, her insight unexpected, her use of a word like love a cruel taunt that reminded him of the absence of positive emotions in his life. Her quick recovery startled him, too, and he realized that he would have to guard against the maturity she'd acquired if they spent much more time together. "You're speculating. Don't waste your time."

"I don't agree, but have it your way for now." She lifted her chin and squared her shoulders. "Thank you for rescuing me. I'm sorry I wasn't able to do the same for you before you were sent to prison."

Shaken by her courage, Craig took his time as he added a second log to the dwindling stack in the fireplace. He dusted the tree bark from his hands as he straightened and met her gaze. Startled by the sadness in her expression, he steeled himself against responding to her vulnerability. "Save your appreciation and pity for someone who wants it."

"I don't pity you," Chelsea insisted. "What I feel is regret."

"How do you intend to repay me?"

She frowned. "For what?"

"Saving your life, of course. In some cultures you'd be obligated to me forever. Interesting concept, don't you think?"

Shifting uneasily, Chelsea's eyes darted from his calculating expression to the front door of the cabin. Craig watched her, his relaxed posture a deceptive cover for his primitive needs. She reminded him of a mouse trapped by a hungry cat, and he could see that she didn't like the feeling any more than he had.

"No glib comebacks, Chelsea? No more psychobabble about high walls?"

Craig remained standing in front of the fireplace as she crossed the room, claimed her sodden purse from the kitchen counter where he'd dropped it earlier, and dug out her wallet. The defiance and fury he saw on her face took him by surprise and reminded him yet again of the changes that had taken place in her in recent years.

"Cash, check, or shall I arrange for a money order?" she asked in a belligerent tone of voice that set off a reaction in Craig that he didn't bother to contain.

He shot across the room like a rocket, his eyes flashing fury as he seized Chelsea by the upper arms. She cried out in surprise, her checkbook flying out of her hand and falling to the floor. He jerked her against his chest and crushed her lips beneath his.

Craig meant to teach her a lesson. He meant to punish her for her flippant attitude, just as he meant to demonstrate his complete dominance over her. But he hadn't counted on being seduced by the taste of her, hadn't anticipated the lush feel of her beneath his hands when he stripped the towel from her struggling body and closed his hands over her full breasts.

She fought him, her lips clamped together, her clenched fists battering his chest. He understood her reaction, even felt grudging respect for it, but he couldn't stop himself from participating in the explosive struggle for control that they'd both set in motion.

He fed on her lips like a wild creature too long deprived of food. He touched her everywhere, shaping her hips, smoothing up and down her narrow back, and stroking the gentle curve of her belly before reclaiming her breasts.

Her hands opened. She gripped his shoulders, her palms pressing, her fingers kneading. Chelsea gasped beneath his mouth. Craig responded to the entrée she provided by plunging his tongue past her parted lips and drinking in her taste. She twisted and turned beneath his hands, setting his loins on fire and threatening his control. He smothered the groan that rose up inside of him, unwilling to reveal the true extent of his need for her.

With a suddenness that caught him off guard, she went absolutely still in his arms. Craig felt the change in her the instant it happened. Rather than question his good fortune, he plundered the hot, sweet interior of her mouth while he continued to fondle her firm breasts. He knew he hadn't ever touched anyone or anything in his entire life that felt so perfectly formed or so sensually volatile.

Chelsea seduced him by simply being herself, and she proved to Craig that the reality of her was better than all the memories of her, no matter how vivid.

She moaned into his mouth, but he heard an absence of protest in the profoundly sensual sound. He felt her nipples stiffen and stab like tiny daggers into his palms. His fingers spasmed, digging into her breasts. Chelsea sighed, the sound ragged. He tasted it, heard it, and recognized it as complete capitulation. Still, he experienced a moment of anxiety at the thought of trusting how willing she'd become.

His need to punish slowly disappeared, while his desire to dominate faded in the shadow of his hunger for her passion. He savored her touch when he felt her hands at his waist, but he nearly stopped breathing when she tugged free the belt that held his robe together, pushed the fabric aside, and burrowed against his hard flesh.

She amazed him, first with her gentleness as she stroked the side of his face with her fingertips, and then when she angled her head and parted her lips for even greater access. He gripped her hips and snugged her closer, the feel of her painful and exquisite. Sensation glittered across his senses like a sky crusted with diamonds. She welcomed the intrusive thrust of his tongue into her mouth, stunning him with her sensuality as she used her swaying hips to shift back and forth against his throbbing maleness.

Sucking at her tongue, Craig savored her sweet taste. He shuddered when she turned the tables on him, captured the tip of his tongue, and worried it with gentle teeth. His heart racing and his body aflame, he couldn't get enough of her, but his reckless hunger suddenly penetrated his consciousness and made him pause.

Releasing her lips, he dragged in enough air to fill his lungs as he threw back his head. Craig tried to think clearly, but he couldn't. He slid his arms around her, unwilling to lose the feel of her pressed so intimately against his aroused body. He listened to the uneven sound of Chelsea's breathing while he brought his own under control.

Several minutes later he muttered a curse. Chelsea flinched. The emotional conflict he felt made him question his sanity. He let go of her.

She didn't try to cover herself. Craig briefly wondered if she even realized that she was naked.

They stared at each other. The flush of her skin and her dazed expression ate at his conscience, but the fever still scorching him refused to allow him to chastise himself for what had just happened between them. Collecting her towel from the floor, he shoved it into her hands and walked away, but the sound of her voice made him pause before he left the room.

"I used to stand in your closet for hours on end when they first took you away," she confessed. "I missed you so much, I thought I'd die from the loneliness, but your clothes let me surround myself with your musky scent. I even wore your T-shirts to bed at night. This probably sounds crazy to you, but it helped me get from one day to the next in the beginning." Chelsea laughed, but the sound trailed into a strangled half sob. "I told myself over and over again that no matter what happened to you, you'd still be the same man when you were finally released from prison. How wrong I was."

Taken aback by her honesty, not just the despair that tinged her words, Craig finally realized that she, too, had paid a price for the hand dealt to them by Fate and her dead father. "That's what I've been trying to tell you."

"I believe you now," she whispered. "I guess the real question is whether or not you're willing to give me the time I need to know the new you."

"Why bother?" he ground out.

"I think you're worth the effort."

"I don't, so forget it."

Chelsea paled. "I hope you'll change your mind, Craig. Besides, I'm not the same person either. We've both got a lot to learn about each other."

He turned slowly, his voice rich with contempt. "I've learned something new about you already. You're definitely a lot hotter these days, babe, and I suspect you're pure dynamite in the sack, but then I always thought you had a lot of potential in that department." He chuckled humorlessly. "Oh, you might want to check out the chest of drawers in the bedroom at the end of the hallway, unless you decide to walk around this place like a full-time proposition while you're here. You'll find sweat suits and blankets, and you'll need both since you're sleeping on the couch tonight."

Chelsea lifted her chin. She earned Craig's reluctant admiration as she stood there, un-

clothed and defiant in the face of his deliberately careless remarks. "What about food?" she
asked. "It's getting late, and I'm hungry."

He nodded in the direction of the kitchen.
"Help yourself."

"Will I be able to leave in the morning?"

"I haven't got a clue."

Craig walked away then, his body still on
fire, his nerves shredded, his emotions in chaos,
and his regret for what they'd lost years earlier
a painful ache in his chest.

FIVE

Unable to sleep even though it was well after midnight, Chelsea gazed at the dying flames of the fire and listened to the rain striking the roof. She felt a kind of soul-deep fatigue, which didn't really surprise her since she'd endured the equivalent of having her emotions run backward through a keyhole. Sighing softly, she adjusted her pillow and shifted atop the lumpy couch cushions in an effort to find a more comfortable position.

An hour passed, but sleep still eluded her. Chelsea sensed Craig's presence before she actually saw him. He moved soundlessly across the semidark room, his body naked except for a pair of jeans. The worn denim molded like a second skin to his powerful legs and rode low on his lean hips, the zipper open to reveal the narrow trail of dark hair that descended from the pelt of coarse silk that covered his wide chest.

As he leaned down to transfer a stack of logs to the fireplace grate, Chelsea held her breath and watched the smooth flex and flow of the muscles woven in an intricate pattern beneath the rich honey color of his skin. He straightened a few moments later, shoving careless fingers through the dense fall of dark hair that had shifted forward across his shoulders.

The dry wood caught and the fire flared. Craig remained in front of the hearth, his head tilted back, his eyes closed, and his hands extended in front of him.

Mesmerized by the perfect lines and fluid grace of his large body, Chelsea hungrily studied him, her senses alive. She yearned to run her fingertips the length and breadth of his form. He glanced her way, and she lowered her lashes to hide the fact that she was awake, while holding very still as she waited for him to return to his bedroom.

He surprised her when he approached her, pausing beside the couch with an intent expression that Chelsea thought would have looked normal on a wild creature studying its prey. After several long moments of silent observation,

Craig dropped down, his knees bent as he balanced on the balls of his bare feet.

She felt her heart stutter with disbelief when he tugged the blanket draped at her waist up and over her chest. He tucked the rough fabric around her shoulders, his hands gentle as they lingered on her upper arms. She exhaled, her lungs burning, but she tried to make the sound an exhalation typical of anyone deep in sleep. All her efforts to conceal her awareness of him ceased, however, when he trailed the tip of his finger down the side of her cheek.

Chelsea stopped breathing altogether. Her eyes snapped open, and she couldn't conceal her shocked response to his caring gesture. She searched the angular lines of his face illuminated by the blazing fire, desperate to understand his behavior. Craig jerked his hand away.

They stared at each other, the crackle of burning logs and the occasional hiss of rainwater leaking down the chimney and landing on the fire the only sounds inside the cabin. Outside, Mother Nature continued her assault, but neither Chelsea nor Craig seemed aware of anything but each other.

She suddenly felt suspended between reality and fantasy. She didn't move a muscle, certain that Craig's earlier hostility would prompt him to reject her if she reached out to him, but she still longed for his embrace. Once again, her gaze skimmed the contours of his hard-cheeked face. She noted the tension that narrowed his dark eyes and made a muscle twitch in his clenched jaw.

She saw something more, though. At least, she *thought* she saw a hint of something more when she glimpsed the vulnerability that flashed in his eyes, but he blinked, reclaiming the disdainful expression that seemed normal now when he looked at her.

Chelsea ached for him. She wanted to gather him close and hold him. She longed to warm his heart and revitalize his damaged spirit. She also wished that she could wave a magic wand and make the past disappear, but she knew she couldn't alter Craig's negative opinion of her or banish their individual memories of the bad experiences endured during the last six years.

"Why aren't you asleep?" he asked.

"I was, briefly. I woke up a little while ago."

"You've had a tough day."

"It was that," she agreed quietly.

She thought then of the dozens of moments of crisis she faced each time she walked into the children's ward at the hospital and donned her volunteer uniform, but her tumble into the flooded ravine had been different. She'd confronted her own mortality for the first time in several years, and it had affected her in ways she couldn't even begin to express.

Chelsea mustered a hesitant smile as she shifted on the couch. She grimaced, though, when a spring jabbed her in the hip.

Craig gave her a wry look. "You don't like the accommodations?"

"The couch is a little lumpy."

"It's a lot lumpy," he said.

She watched his eyes darken with emotions she couldn't identify. "My body's tired and bruised, but my thoughts are still running a hundred miles an hour."

Before Craig could respond, thunder boomed across the night sky. It rattled the windows while the wind howled. Chelsea glanced uneasily at a nearby window. She saw lightning streak across the dark sky.

"The storm doesn't sound like it's easing at all." Without any warning, she remembered the wall of water that had swept her off the bridge and into the ravine. Shivering, she knew that her delayed reaction to the event wasn't abnormal, but she felt unsettled just the same.

"We aren't in danger of flooding, Chelsea," he said, as though reading her thoughts. "The cabin's on high ground." As he spoke, Craig slid down to a seated position on the floor, his long legs stretched out in front of him and crossed at the ankles, his back against the couch; he stared at the flames ribboning around the logs he'd added a few minutes earlier. "Do you need to talk about today?" he asked.

She found his compassion unexpected . . . and appreciated. "I probably do, if you don't mind listening. I thought I was going to die in that ravine. I've only felt that way once before." Chelsea kept her voice even, unwilling to reveal the incident she referred to. It would be a case of too much said too soon. "It's not a good feeling."

"Your only option is to let go of the memory. It'll fade with time."

She nodded. "That's what I want to do, but I see myself falling in slow motion when I least expect the image to pop into my head."

"I understand," he said in a low voice.

She knew in her heart that he understood all too well about threatening situations. "What are you thinking about?"

He shrugged. "Nothing important."

She hesitated, her gaze roaming his profile and then the mane of dark hair that swept back from his high forehead and flowed down past his broad shoulders. She thought he looked primitive, like a throwback to a lost culture where the men were dominant and untamed. She sighed softly as her hungry gaze moved down across his wide chest and flat belly. She still couldn't quite grasp the changes in his physique. Muscular, hard, but resilient-looking, too, his body appeared to have been sculpted by an artist who specialized in the male form.

"You're staring, Chelsea."

She blinked, then flushed. "I am, aren't I, but can you really blame me? Your body looks so different, so . . . powerful."

His voice level, he said, "Working out helped pass the time and lower my frustration level."

"And it made a statement about your ability to defend yourself."

The muscle at the top of his jaw started to pulse again. Glancing at her, he pondered her features for several seconds, then redirected his attention to the fire. "When did you become an authority on what motivates a con?"

She sighed, hating the way he referred to himself as a *con*. She vowed in that moment to find a way to help him stop labeling himself as anything but a man.

"Have you forgotten that I tried to visit you twice a month for the first year?" she asked. "I know you were told each time I arrived, because you refused to see me. I used to wait in the visitor's building, which was an educational experience I didn't exactly want, but I got it anyway. I saw the way the men traveled in packs, even when their families were there, and I noticed the menacing look, the look that said confront-me-at-your-own-risk, in the eyes of men who obviously worked out in the prison gym. I also read some books suggested by the warden, just in case . . ." She knew she'd already admitted too much when he peered at her, so she paused.

"In case what?" Craig pressed.

"I didn't know if you'd want me to be a part of your readjustment once you were released, but I wanted to be prepared to help if you did." She watched him close his hands into white-knuckled fists atop his muscular thighs. Looking quickly away, she asked, "Didn't you miss me at all, Craig?"

He stiffened, as though readying himself for a blow. He glared at her, muttered a curse, and stared again into the fire. She watched his struggle for control while her heart raced.

"I'm sorry. I shouldn't pry."

He exhaled, the sound oddly strained. "I tried not to think about the past. It's unproductive to dwell on things you can't change. And if the people around you think you aren't alert to the threat they pose to you twenty-four hours a day, you can end up dead."

"I can't imagine having to be on guard all the time."

"It's the most important job a man has in prison."

"But what about the things you can change now?"

"They don't exist."

"You're wrong. The evidence I brought—"

"I'm not interested in the past," he interrupted.

Change the subject, Chelsea told herself. "Why did you decide to live here?"

"The property's mine."

"But why?" She raised herself up on one elbow. "You're all alone. No friends or neighbors, according to your parole officer."

"I need the space."

"Aren't you really saying that you don't want to risk trusting anyone with your emotions? Or is it that you don't trust yourself around so-called normal people yet?"

"You're walking a dangerous line."

She forged ahead, instinctively unable to give up on him. "It's a risk I'm willing to take."

"Drop it, Chelsea. Now," he ordered sharply.

"I can't. You deserve my efforts, and you need a friend."

He shot a scathing look at her. "You're the last person on this planet worthy of my trust. The very last."

"Give me a chance to prove to you that you're wrong about me. Come to San Francisco for a visit."

"I didn't forget anything when I left there six years ago."

You forgot me, she longed to tell him, but said instead, "Consider a visit. Do you remember the wonderful food at that Szechuan restaurant at Ghirardelli Square? If you don't want to eat out, we could pack a picnic and go sailing, or see a play, or maybe even visit old friends."

"Why bother?"

"You might be surprised by how much you'd enjoy yourself."

"Don't plan my life for me, Chelsea. I've had my fill of people doing that kind of thing."

"I wouldn't plan anything, unless you asked, of course." She slid her hand across his shoulder. "I swear I wouldn't do anything you didn't want me to do, Craig."

He shrugged free of her touch. Leaning forward, he looped his arms around his upraised knees. "I can't handle crowds yet."

She could see what his admission cost him, especially given the man he'd once been. "The bay isn't very crowded early in the morning."

"You actually kept the boat."

"I wouldn't sell your sailboat. You loved it. Jack Sinclair's got it in dry dock. It's waiting for you." *Just like me*, she thought. *Just like me.*

Chelsea flipped back the blanket, pushed up from the pillow, and swung her legs over the side of the couch. She eased down to the braided oval rug beside Craig. She positioned her body at an angle so that she could see his face.

Be patient and gentle, she counseled herself as she lifted her hand and slid it across his shoulder. She knew she couldn't lose sight of the fact that he'd been treated like an animal, nor could she forget that he'd learned to respond as one when challenged.

Although she felt the tension that seized him when she touched him, Chelsea ignored it in favor of fingering the long hair that trailed past his shoulders. She understood the risk involved in touching him, but she fully intended to break through the wall of anger and suspicion he'd built around himself.

"I never thought I'd see you with long hair. I like it, although it makes you look amazingly uncivilized."

He remained as still as a statue. She wove her fingers through the long, bluntly cut strands, loving the coarse feel of them on her skin.

Craig caught her wrist, the heat of his hand igniting her senses even more, his grip firm but not hurtful as he eased her fingers away from his hair. "You're playing with fire. If you want to have sex, say so. I might even oblige you, but on my terms."

Chelsea felt the sharp sting of his sarcasm, but she quelled the defensive retort trembling on her tongue. And she didn't pull away, although he had her tilted forward at an odd angle as he held her hand atop his thigh. She wanted his touch, despite his harsh words. She also wanted him to rediscover and trust the tender, more vulnerable side of his personality. She wiggled forward so that her knees pressed against his hard thigh.

"What are you trying to prove?" he demanded.

"Nothing. I'm curious, but I'm definitely not shopping for sex, Craig."

He unshackled her wrist and pushed her hand aside. "I'm not an exhibit in a sideshow, so don't touch me unless I issue an invitation."

"Someday soon, I'll convince you that I don't have a hidden agenda. Until then, I'll be as patient as I know how to be."

"Don't do me any damn favors."

They sat there, eyes locked, measuring each other's strength of will until Craig scowled and looked away. She watched him watch the fire, and she sensed from his stoic expression and rigid body that his thoughts were mired in the chaos of their shared past. She let the minutes tick by, hopeful that Craig would feel relaxed enough again to continue talking in spite of the late hour. She realized that his questions, not just his answers, held the potential of providing her with the means to get beyond his hostile attitude.

"You paid the taxes on this place, didn't you?" he finally asked.

"Yes."

"Did you expect to claim the land and the cabin for yourself?"

Chelsea corralled her temper, despite his scathing tone and his implication that she'd been motivated solely by self-interest. "I didn't want you to lose it. Before he died, your grandfather told me that this property's been owned by your family since the late 1880s. I assumed that you wouldn't want your heritage claimed by the state for nonpayment of taxes."

"You were with him at the end."

She realized that he wasn't asking, but stating a fact he seemed certain of. That he even knew about her time with Ben surprised her, but she didn't mind because she had nothing to hide. "He asked for me when his doctor had him transferred to Memorial in San Francisco for experimental surgery. I stopped in to see him whenever I had time."

"Every day for four months."

Startled, she asked, "How . . . I mean . . . who told you?"

"I spoke to him from prison before he died."

"Oh."

"He appreciated what you did for him."

"I still miss Ben. He was a wonderful man. We played cards when he was strong enough, and every once in a while I'd let him talk me into bringing him a hot fudge sundae from the hospital cafeteria."

"Did you mean what you said before about . . . standing in my closet?"

Startled by his abrupt shift in subjects, Chelsea hesitated. She felt her cheeks flood with color, and she appreciated the semidark condition of the room. "That's not the kind of thing a woman lies about, Craig."

"I find it difficult to believe."

She stared at him, baffled by his need to cling to such a negative image of her. "That I missed you? That even though I knew I couldn't fix what had happened to us, I still needed you in my life? I wanted you in those days more than I wanted air to breathe. It took me a long time, but I eventually recovered and started living my life again. I had no other choice."

"You were innocent when we were first together."

She laughed softly. "Not for very long." Chelsea remembered the attraction that had drawn them together like magnets. She also recalled the awkwardness of their first date, because she'd been the boss's daughter.

"Despite your innocence, you were instinctively sensual."

She felt her pulse pick up speed. "You made me feel things I'd never felt before," Chelsea whispered.

"Did you mind?"

She glanced at him, her uncertainty about his

motives returning. Although uneasy, she found the courage to be honest. "I loved every moment we shared."

"You surprised me today," Craig admitted, his tone less combative. "You're stronger than I ever thought you'd be. You never used to fight back when someone hurt your feelings or challenged your point of view." He shifted. Their knees met, and he studied her with a genuine curiosity.

"I'm older, and I've had the benefit of experiences. Some good, some bad. I had to learn how to take care of myself and articulate my needs."

"With other men?"

Sensitive in the extreme about her nonexistent social life, Chelsea refused to admit that the few dates she'd had were absolute disasters. Her pride wouldn't let her tell anyone that she'd invariably compared every man she met to Craig, and they all fell short. "That's not a question I'm willing to answer, and you have no right to ask it. I'm sure, though, that you'll draw your own conclusions on the subject."

"You're healthy, attractive, and you aren't married."

"So are several hundred thousand other women in California."

"I'm not talking about other women. We're discussing you."

"You're trying to discuss something I don't want to talk about," she corrected. She exhaled, gathering up the reins of her temper before she lost it. "When I said I'd changed, that doesn't have to mean that I accosted every man I encountered, now does it?"

"You tell me." His dark eyes were alive with suspicion.

"I shouldn't have to tell you. You should already know." Chelsea reached out and stroked the side of his face, the stubble from his beard grazing her fingertips and sending sensation streaming up her fingers and into her palm. Craig jerked out of reach. She reluctantly lowered her hand to her lap.

She didn't flinch as his eyes drilled into her, his anger obvious. Although there were things she needed to tell him, Chelsea knew this wasn't the time. "If you feel inclined to judge me," she said with quiet dignity, "then do it based on things that are indisputable, not speculative. I don't deserve that kind of close-mindedness from you. I never did." She stopped herself then, aware that she risked going too far if she lost control of herself.

"What do you think you deserve from me?" Craig asked, his voice unexpectedly subdued.

"Exactly what you deserve from me and everyone else. A fair hearing, not a judgment based on preconceived notions that condemn a person out of hand."

"Fair! The whole concept of fairness is a philosophical illusion."

"You're wrong," she flared. "You have the power to make it mean something, but only if you're willing to make the emotional sacrifice of confronting the past head-on. Read the journal I brought with me, and then we can discuss the concept of fairness."

He eyed her with what almost appeared to be grudging respect. "You're older, you're stronger, and you've got a hell of a temper now, but you're still too naive for the real world, Chelsea."

She leaned forward, grabbed his hands, and held on to him with all her strength. "The world's not a totally evil place. There are kind and loving people all around you, but you have to let yourself recognize them so that you can welcome them into your life. If you give up on the world, then you're giving up on yourself. I refuse to let you do that."

Chelsea kept their hands joined. She studied the emotions crossing his face: Stunned reaction to her intensity, a flash of hope that disappeared almost immediately, skepticism. She held her breath as she watched him, then exhaled shakily when he blinked and reverted to the wary gaze of a cornered animal.

Chelsea wanted to cry, but she placed a stranglehold on her emotions. Releasing his hands, she lifted her fingertips to her temples, closed her eyes, and massaged her temples while she struggled for a calm she doubted she would ever feel again.

"I want to taste you," Craig said a few moments later. He placed his hands, palms down, with fingers extended and spread wide, on her thighs.

Caught off guard by his bluntness, Chelsea met his gaze. She felt the warmth of his touch seep into her skin, his hands branding her despite the thick material of the sweatpants she wore. Torn between her hunger for him and her fear of being used, she stared at him. Her heart pounded.

His fingers dug into her thighs. "I *need* another taste of you, Chelsea."

She realized he was waiting for her to make the next move. She trusted her instincts and banished her common sense to a quiet alcove in the back of her mind.

"Then taste me," she invited as she strained forward.

He gathered her into his arms and shifted her onto his lap. Chelsea slipped her fingers across his shoulders, up the sides of his muscular neck, and then drove them into his mane of hair. Pressing her fingers against his warm scalp, she kneaded like a she-cat who'd finally found her mate.

Craig edged forward, brushing his lips back and forth over hers until she nearly wept with surprise and pleasure. This was the old Craig, she realized. The tender, teasing lover she'd missed so desperately.

Her eyes closed in the next instant as he took her lips with a gentleness that stunned her. She trembled in his embrace, her lips parting on a sharp intake of breath, her fingers tangling in his long hair.

His tongue darted forward to stroke her wet inner lip. Her senses sparkled with sensations too wide-ranging to name. As he sampled her sweetness, Chelsea simultaneously drank in his taste, her own hunger intensifying at a reckless pace.

Craig followed her lead, his lips nibbling, his tongue taunting as it dipped in and out of her mouth. He initiated an erotic duel that left Chelsea breathless and clinging to him. She gloried in his hunger for her, but she also sensed in his sensually explicit kisses the loneliness and pain that had ruled his life for so many years.

She felt her heart lurch painfully beneath her ribs before she sidestepped the realities that she feared would always haunt him. She inhaled his groans, welcomed the heat emanating from his half-naked body, and adored the consuming sweep of his hands as they traveled up and down her back.

Pressed against his chest, her unrestrained breasts firmed and peaked, the sweatshirt she wore a meaningless barrier in the path of her feverish response to him. She squirmed closer, circling his hips with her slender legs. Their loins met, and she heard the deep groan that rumbled from his chest. She felt the narrow ridge of flesh straining beneath his unfastened jeans. Instinct guiding her yet again, Chelsea reached for him, but Craig caught her hand and held it away from his arousal.

He dragged his mouth free of hers, his breathing choppy as he shifted her backward so that she wound up straddling his thighs. She moaned in protest, desire and need streaming through her, but he contained her twisting body with hands fixed firmly at her waist so that she couldn't move until and unless he allowed it.

"What's wrong?" she asked, breathless and on fire for him.

"You taste sweet." He uttered the words like an accusation.

Confused, she studied his features. She knew he desired her. She'd felt it, tasted it, and now she craved more of it.

Feeling brave, she closed her fingers around his wrists and guided his hands beneath the loose shirt he'd loaned to her. She watched his eyes darken with intensity as she slowly brought his palms up her midriff and into contact with her breasts. She molded his big hands over her aching flesh, gasping at the sensations that ribboned through her senses.

Craig hissed a raw curse, his fingers spasming as he possessively cupped her silky flesh, but he released her just seconds later. She called out his name in dismay.

He surged to his feet without warning, Chelsea molded against his chest. He dumped her onto the couch and turned to face the fire. She tumbled back across the lumpy cushions, her jaw going slack with shock as she stared at him. Because of the poor illumination in the room, she didn't recognize the scars crisscrossing his lower back for what they were until several minutes passed. A growing sense of horror, coupled with her disbelief that he'd been subjected to physical assaults by other inmates, engulfed her.

"Craig . . ." she began hesitantly.

"Don't say another word," he warned. "It'll only get you into trouble."

Chelsea scrambled into a seated position and yanked her sweatshirt into place. "Talk to me, please. I don't understand what's happening."

Cynicism etched his angular features when he finally turned to look at her. Her gaze dropped to his groin, then lifted to his face. She knew he still wanted her, but his blazing eyes said otherwise. She froze, uncertainty streaming through her, paralyzing her.

"That's right, Chelsea. My body's still on fire for you. You're very good. What was the plan? Give the poor sex-starved bastard anything he wants, and he'll be your devoted slave forever? Forget it, because I meant it when I said we'd have sex only on my terms."

Sagging under his cruelty, she lacked the strength to defend herself even though she felt the impulse rising up inside herself like an angry shout. Controlling her emotions and keeping her voice level, she pointed out, "You started this, Craig. Not me."

"And now I'm finishing it." He walked away from her without another word, chilling her right down to her soul.

Still in shock and shaking badly in the aftermath of his contempt, Chelsea nursed her pain as she burrowed beneath the blanket. She tried to understand what she'd done wrong, but her thoughts were too scattered for coherent reasoning. She also tried to come to terms with the brutality Craig had encountered in prison, but she lacked even the most basic comprehension of why people inflicted their rage on others in the first place.

She eventually managed to fall asleep, but dreams from the past haunted her throughout the rest of the night. The storm worsened, and in those long, lonely hours before dawn, Chelsea resigned herself to the fact that Craig Wilder would never again trust her with his love.

SIX

Craig held a book, but he couldn't concentrate on reading it. The stillness of his body and the unrevealing expression on his face masked his discontent at being trapped indoors by the weather. Sprawled on the couch in front of the fireplace, he watched Chelsea pace from window to window.

She'd been in motion on and off for most of the morning. He noted her white-knuckled grip on the mug of coffee she held and the deep frown on her face.

She paused, peering out the window nearest the front door at the wind-whipped trees, flattened shrubs, and driving rain. Thunder boomed, then an almost breathless kind of stillness settled over the cabin. She stood quietly, as though preparing herself for the next blast of sound.

Craig heard the anxious sigh that escaped Chelsea just moments later. His nerves knotted even more tightly and his annoyance escalated when she started walking again.

"You remind me of a cat that's been dropped onto a hot griddle. Why don't you sit down and relax before you wear a path in the floor?"

Chelsea ignored him, her footsteps soundless as she moved to the window next to a battered bookcase. Once again, she peered outside. Craig wondered if she recognized the plot of freshly turned, saturated earth located just outside the window as the site for the garden he intended to plant in the spring. Gardening. The only useful skill he'd acquired in prison, he reflected bitterly.

Craig gripped his well-thumbed paperback, his irritation with her behavior finally bursting free. "Chelsea!"

She paused briefly, then resumed her pacing. "I can't stop. How can you just sit there like a lump? Why don't you do something?"

"Exactly what did you have in mind?" Craig sat up and shifted his feet to the floor.

He understood that Chelsea felt trapped by circumstances beyond her control. He also knew how unsettling that feeling could be, but he reminded himself that she'd known little adversity in her pampered, only-child life. She deserved to learn that she couldn't control every aspect of her life, as well as to experience the humiliation that often accompanied that lesson.

Chelsea paused in the center of the room. Craig glimpsed uncertainty, wariness, and a healthy measure of suspicion in her eyes as she studied him. Clad in an old flannel shirt that trailed past her knees and a pair of woolen socks, she looked young and vulnerable and too sexy for words.

Desire lanced through him, reminding him of the lightning bolts that had zigzagged through the heavens the night before. Caught by surprise, he stiffened and fought the heat searing his veins and flooding his loins.

"You're the expert on living out in the boonies," Chelsea remarked. "Don't you have any ideas about how I can get out of here?"

He smiled, a hard little smile. "Do I make you nervous?"

She paled. "Hardly."

"Then what's your problem?"

"I need to get back to the city. I have things to do."

"Like what?" he asked, curious in spite of himself. "A charity luncheon, a stroll through an art gallery to kill an afternoon, or maybe one of those tedious fashion shows you used to love so much. You really need to get a life, Chelsea."

"I have a life," she snapped. "Despite what you'd like to believe, I'm not some frivolous twit who wanders around and waits for people to amuse me."

"Right," he said derisively.

She crossed the room, lingering in front of the fireplace. "Do you have a radio? I'd like to hear the weather forecast."

"The batteries are dead."

Chelsea glanced at him. "What about a phone? Couldn't we call the weather service?" Her expression brightened suddenly. "A friend of mine has a helicopter service in Sacramento. I could call and ask her to fly in once the weather clears."

"Forget it. The lines are down."

She frowned. "How is it that we still have power for the lights, the refrigerator, and the coffee maker?"

"Generator," he muttered.

"Is there another route out of here?"

He thought about the old logging trail for a moment. "It isn't safe," he announced.

Her disappointment replaced the spark of optimism his hesitation had caused. "Are you sure?"

"Would I lie to you?"

"If it suited your purposes," she responded, her voice ringing with certainty.

He chuckled humorlessly. Once again, Craig was reminded that she'd changed. She'd grown more talented at reading people. "You're getting suspicious in your old age."

"I've got a brain that works, and you taught me a lesson last night that I'm not about to forget."

He tensed, still angry with himself for believing that she'd really wanted him. "And what lesson was that?"

"You don't deserve my trust."

"And I don't trust you. I guess that puts us on a level playing field, doesn't it?" he asked, no longer inclined to hide his cynicism about her motives.

"There's nothing level about this playing field, and you know it as well as I do. Until you stop blaming me for everything that's gone wrong with your life, we haven't got a prayer of dealing honestly with each other." Her expression dismissive, Chelsea resumed her pacing.

Craig studied her, his eyes narrowed, his

expression brooding. His conscience nudged him, but he refused to accept the fact that she might be right. He dropped the paperback onto the floor a few minutes later, abandoning his morning-long pretense of reading a story that bored him to tears. "Perhaps you need to learn something else."

She didn't even break stride in her wandering from one window to the next. "You don't have anything to teach me that I'm interested in learning, so save your breath."

"I'm good at waiting, Chelsea," he reminded her. "Very good."

Her footsteps faltered, her eyes darting to his face and then skittering away. "You're comparing apples to oranges."

"No. I'm telling you that being stuck in this cabin for a day or two with me doesn't even begin to compare to six years in a prison cell."

Chelsea glared at him.

"Settle down and settle in," he advised coldly. "Take a nap or read a book. I don't care. This storm isn't letting up, so be glad you aren't out in it."

"I'm fine the way I am, so quit treating me like some fool who hasn't got the sense God gave a rock."

"You're acting like an overly tired three-year-old on the verge of a tantrum." He grinned, then suggested, "If you want to do something useful, why don't you make lunch?"

"Stop baiting me. I'm tired of it. And you can fix your own lunch. I'm not the maid."

"Then entertain me."

"Entertain you? Sorry," she said, clearly unapologetic. "I don't dance, sing, or tell jokes."

"Why don't you tell me about the men in your life? I'm sure that would be very entertaining."

She paused beside the bar that separated the kitchen from the main room. Placing her coffee mug on the countertop with care, she pressed her palms together in front of her chest, turned to face him, and cautiously peered at him. "Tell you about the what?"

"The men, Chelsea. The ones who've taught you so much since I've been away. I'm curious to know if they appreciated the fact that I . . . broke you in, or don't I count since I'm just an ex-con?"

"You're crazy!"

"I don't think so, and if your response to me last night was any indication, you don't either." He surged to his feet. "*You* liked it when I touched you last night. *You* put my hands on your breasts. *You* squirmed in my lap and tried to crawl under my skin. *You* moaned into my mouth. And *you* writhed with the pleasure you felt, so don't try to deny the obvious."

"The obvious?" She was deathly pale.

"You're hotter than a firecracker, babe. That kind of responsiveness comes from lots of practice between the sheets."

She sighed, the sound filled with so many emotions that Craig couldn't identify them all. Hands clenched at his sides, he pinned her in place with a harsh look when she started to take a step. She hesitated, clearly weighing her limited options. He watched her struggle between standing her ground or fleeing, and he also assumed that much of the inner conflict revealed in her expressive eyes was based on her discomfort with admitting the truth.

"All right, Craig, I'll tell you everything you want to know." Chelsea squared her shoulders and lifted her chin, defiance suddenly blazing in her hazel eyes. "I guess I should start with Howard Lacey. He's an architect, and he loves the theater. We go out several times a month."

"What else does he love?" Craig demanded.

She smiled, the epitome of the poised San Francisco debutante she'd once been. "The shape of my thighs, so I always wear short dresses for Howard. And then, of course, there's Marty Doherty."

"He's married to your best friend."

Her expression bland, she said, "So?"

He forced his next comment past his disbelief. "You're sleeping with married men?"

Chelsea shrugged carelessly. "Everyone does it. Besides, they rarely kiss and tell." She tapped a finger against her chin, then smiled like a cat about to savor a dish of cream. "Oh, we can't forget Tom Lansberg. He's an old friend of my father's. Tom's a sweetheart, although he's twenty years my senior and we have to . . . pace ourselves. Tom's going to run in the next mayoral race, and he likes to have me with him whenever he's interviewed by the media. You might even remember him, since he attended our wedding."

Stunned, Craig watched her smooth back the curly tendrils of auburn hair that had drifted across her cheek. He felt like wringing her neck.

"To be honest, though, I think my favorite is Jim Marshall. He won a seat in Congress in the last election, and he loves to play tennis, which you know is my favorite game. Shall I continue?"

Craig feigned calm. "You're lying to me."

"Am I? Prove it."

He felt his self-control unravel in the face of her belligerence. "Why?" he demanded, his voice sounding like a long stretch of gravel road.

"You said you wanted to be entertained, so don't complain when I give you exactly what you asked for. Think about it, Craig. Now you can feel self-righteous as all hell when you treat me like some awful creature without morals or values. You should thank me, because I've done what you couldn't do. I've justified your miserable suspicions about my morality—or lack of it. Why don't you splurge and send me flowers as a remembrance of this truly special occasion?"

"You make yourself sound like a slut."

"The only person who's ever made me feel that way is you. Are we finished with this idiotic conversation?"

She didn't try to escape him as he advanced on her. If anything, Craig realized that she intended to confront him when she raised her chin and closed her graceful hands into small fists at her sides.

He grabbed her by the shoulders and jerked her forward. She slammed against his chest, but she met his furious gaze with a look of pure stubbornness in her eyes that amazed him.

For a brief moment, Craig actually realized that he should apologize to her for what he'd just put her through. He hesitated, though, weighing the possibility of an apology against his desire to make her pay for her betrayal.

His conscience reminded him that he could have her off his land in a matter of hours by using the road that led into a nearby valley, but he felt compelled to keep her cooped up in his cabin for a few days, even if she tried to drive him nuts with jealousy. He reasoned that isolating her was modest retribution for the years he'd spent languishing in a prison cell not much larger than a coffin.

"*Have* you been with other men, Chelsea?"

"I made it clear last night that I wouldn't answer that question. I meant what I said."

Craig gripped her shoulders, a tremor of fury moving through his big body. He felt physically ill at the thought of other men touching her, tasting her, seducing her into their beds. "Answer me."

She glanced beyond him, her gaze lingering for a moment on the journal abandoned the day before on the table and still waiting for his attention. "Read my father's journal, and I'll think about giving you an answer."

"Chelsea." His low, lethal-sounding voice, his entire demeanor, shouted warning. "You're not in any position to make deals."

"I'm not participating any further in this war you've decided to wage against me, so stop needling me. And for the record, Craig Wilder, I was serious when I told you I'm strong enough to handle you. You don't have a clue about what I've been through during the last six years. Since you haven't cared enough to ask, do not make the mistake of underestimating me."

His shock and anger loosened his hold on her and gave her the opportunity to wrench free of his hands. Chelsea ducked out of reach when he made a grab for her. She darted into the kitchen, pausing on the opposite side of the bar, a mutinous expression on her face.

Craig no longer trusted himself. He charged across the room and headed outside, slamming the door behind him. He left his slicker and shotgun in the cabin.

Oblivious to the fury of the thunderstorm, he walked off his anger with a determined stride and clenched fists that he occasionally pounded against a tree trunk or a fence post. He didn't feel the cold or the wet as he struggled with the images teeming in his mind of Chelsea sprawled naked across the beds of other men.

Craig prowled the surrounding terrain for more than an hour. He finally calmed down enough to return to the cabin. Stripping off his soaked clothes, he toweled dry and then stepped into jeans and put on a shirt that he didn't bother to button.

As he brushed his thick wet hair off his face and left it to dry naturally, he discarded the idea of forcing Chelsea to do penance for her betrayal and focused on trying to forget that she'd once been the most important person in his life.

Chelsea stiffened when she heard the front door slam. As she resumed stirring the chicken noodle soup, she heard Craig's booted footsteps crossing the main room of the cabin. She breathed a sigh of relief when he entered his bedroom and closed the door behind him. Lowering the flame beneath the pan, she replaced the lid and left the soup to simmer.

Turning her attention to the sandwiches she'd assembled during Craig's absence, Chelsea vowed to keep her temper under control when, and if, he decided to join her for lunch. She then searched the cupboards for a tray.

His meager supply of cracked dishes and scarred glasses reminded her of the crystal and china they'd used for both hurried breakfasts and lingering romantic meals at the end of Craig's workday. With a sigh, Chelsea set aside her memories when she spotted a serving tray on the top shelf of the cupboard.

Dragging a stool across the room, she muttered under her breath about the inconvenience of being too blasted short for her own good. She climbed atop it, steadying herself with one hand against the wall.

"What the hell are you doing?"

She jerked in surprise, then twisted to find Craig standing in the doorway of the small kitchen. "Fixing lunch."

"Get down from there," he ordered as he approached her.

"I couldn't reach the—"

Her explanation died on a sharp intake of breath when he seized her by the waist and pulled her off the rickety stool. Eyes riveted on his face, Chelsea grabbed his shoulders as he slowly slid her down the front of his body. She felt every muscular inch of his naked chest. Her shirt rode up, exposing her skin to the cold metal snap of his jeans as it traced a line up the soft swell of her belly.

He paused, his body trembling. He held her suspended above the floor, their eyes level. They stared at each other. She inhaled shakily, breathing in the scent of the raindrops that lingered in his hair. As she fought the urge to wrap her legs around his hips, she felt the press of his hardening loins against the cradle of her upper thighs. His potent maleness sent her senses into a riot of reaction.

In self-defense, she said the first thing that tumbled into her mind. "Did you have a nice walk?"

Craig released her. She dropped to the floor, dizzy in the aftermath of such close contact. Smoothing her shirt into place with shaking hands, she avoided his gaze once she found the strength to step away from him.

Craig got the serving tray and placed it beside the sandwiches stacked on the breadboard. He slouched against the counter edge, his arms crossed over his broad chest, his gaze cold and hard.

Chelsea nervously sliced and then transferred the ham-and-cheese sandwiches to a platter, which she set on the tray. Adding utensils, dishes, bowls, and napkins, she held her tongue, even though she wanted to chastise Craig for treating her like a thief.

After rinsing her hands at the sink, she crossed the kitchen and stepped into a long, narrow room designed to function as a laundry room and makeshift pantry. A low-wattage bulb provided minimal illumination. Still shaken by Craig's aggressive behavior, she paused for a moment to collect herself before she searched the shelves for the can of peaches she'd spotted earlier. She nearly dropped the can when she turned to exit the windowless room and saw Craig.

He filled the doorway, blocking out the light from the kitchen. Chelsea felt as though a predator had stalked and cornered her. She hesitated, fighting the panic she felt before she forced herself to move forward as if nothing was amiss. Faking a level of confidence she doubted she'd ever felt in her entire life, she said, "Please move out of the way."

Craig moved forward instead. Chelsea froze. He towered over her, and she felt even smaller than usual. When he relieved her of the can of peaches, she didn't try to stop him. He slid the can onto a nearby shelf, his eyes never leaving her face as she stared up at him.

"I won't be intimidated by you or any other man, and I refuse to play power games with you, so let me pass."

"This isn't a game anymore, Chelsea."

He took a step forward.

She backed up.

He took another step.

She paled, but she kept her expression neutral as she edged backward an additional two steps.

He kept coming at her. He didn't stop, not even when she bumped into the rear wall of the pantry.

Chelsea pressed her open palms against the wall, but she schooled her features to indifference to conceal her anxiety.

He eliminated the few inches that still separated them. She felt his heat and strength as he aligned his body to the soft curves of her smaller one.

She peered up at him, her breathing shallow. She tried to understand his motives, but his once-expressive eyes told her nothing of his thoughts.

He lifted his hand to her cheek. She couldn't keep herself from flinching. Craig frowned, his hand poised just a few inches from her face. He looked to her like a man in search of vengeance. Did he even have a conscience any longer? she wondered. "What are you trying to prove?" she finally asked.

"I don't have to prove anything to you, Chelsea."

She trembled, and closed her eyes. She felt the glide of his fingertips down her cheek, then his thumb as he gently traced the fullness of her lower lip. She sighed. He muttered a curse. Her eyes snapped open, revealing desire . . . and confusion.

"You want me. Why don't you admit it?" he demanded.

"No!" she cried, bringing her fists up to his bare chest.

He edged even closer, his swollen loins nudging her belly as he slid his leg between her thighs. "Be honest with me. Just this once."

"I am being honest."

Unable to stop herself, she opened her hands and flattened them against his chest. She immediately felt the furious beating of his heart and the warmth of his skin as she sank her fingers into the coarse silk that covered his chest. She nearly moaned from the pleasure of touching him. When she heard him suck in his breath, she kneaded the muscled flesh beneath her fingertips with catlike finesse.

"I'm going to touch you the way I used to," he told her in a voice made raw by desire. "You always liked it when I used my hands and mouth on you, Chelsea."

She twisted against him in soundless protest, but her thoughtless movement brought them into even closer contact. Chelsea recalled his

DON'T HOLD BACK!

1. No obligation! No purchase necessary! Enter our Sweepstakes for a chance to win!
2. FREE! Get your first shipment of 6 Loveswept books, *and* a lighted makeup case as a free gift.
3. Save money! Become a member and about once a month you get 6 books for the price of 4! Return any shipment you don't want.
4. Be the first! You'll always receive your Loveswept books before they are available in stores. You'll be the first to thrill to these exciting new stories.

Detach here and mail today.

Give in to love and see where passion leads you!
Enter the Winners Classic Sweepstakes and
send for your FREE lighted makeup case and
6 FREE Loveswept books today!

(See details inside.)

Detach here and mail today.

ability to rid her of any and all inhibitions while skillfully reducing her to a seething mass of fiery sensations. She feared his seduction, because she knew that he simply meant to use her, not make love to her.

"I used to hear the sounds you made in my dreams. You'd purr your pleasure when we had sex. I want you to do that for me again."

Chelsea couldn't speak. She shook her head, then quivered violently as he shifted and suggestively rubbed the long, hard ridge of his arousal against her abdomen. She struggled to remain passive when he pressed his denim-covered thigh against the thin silk of her panties.

"Don't do this to me," she begged, her knees weak, her insides quickening with need.

"Don't do what?" he asked. "Don't make you want me? Don't force you to remember what you helped destroy? Don't stoke the fires burning inside you because they might get out of control and burn you? Which is it, Chelsea?"

She felt pure terror streak into her heart as she stared up at him. Terror because she wanted him so desperately. Terror because she still loved him beyond anyone or anything in the world. Terror because she would always love him, whether or not he loved her back.

The fierce desire in his eyes paralyzed her

for a moment. Seconds later she shivered, her nipples tightening into hard buds that craved his sucking mouth. She breathed raggedly, the muscles in her body as tense and tightly strung as piano wires.

Closing her eyes, Chelsea pressed her head back against the wall, unable to speak, unable to reason clearly, unable to do anything but respond to the reality that she'd waited six long years to experience the full force of Craig's passion again.

Her resistance began to crumble when she felt the glide of his fingertip across the seam of her lips. She reacted on a purely instinctive level, capturing it between her teeth and sucking it into her mouth.

Craig muttered a word that would have sounded ugly under other circumstances, but it slid past his lips like a whispered prayer. Chelsea opened her eyes, no longer willing to hide the desire she felt. In that instant, she consciously abandoned her fear of Craig and her trepidation about the consequences of intimacy between them. Whatever the price, she knew in her heart that she was destined, and more than willing now, to pay it.

Craig became her focus, the center of her existence as she brought both of his hands to her face and pressed them against her cheeks. She nuzzled his palms and fingers, whispering kisses over the callused skin until his hands shook and he pulled them free.

"You were right," she confessed as she looked up at him and viewed the disbelief reflected in his eyes. "I always loved it when you touched me."

Craig covered her breasts with possessive hands. Chelsea arched into his touch, her nipples aching points of need. She craved the feel of his mouth and hands—everywhere, anywhere, and for as long as he could make the pleasure last.

She watched his eyes darken as he molded and shaped her breasts, and she saw the ruddy color that stained his high cheekbones. She felt heat dart into the depths of her body, explode, and then send ever-expanding waves of sensation rippling out from her core.

Craig fumbled with the buttons of her shirt, but he grew impatient within seconds and simply jerked it apart. Fabric tore and buttons bounced every which way as he tugged the shirt off her shoulders, but instead of stripping it from her arms, he shackled her hands behind her back by twisting the fabric around her wrists.

Head spinning and her body trembling with anticipation, Chelsea didn't try to free herself despite how exposed and vulnerable she felt.

She peered up at Craig, dazed and uncertain. She felt like a captive, and she prayed that he wouldn't turn her into a sacrifice on the altar of his rage.

His gaze seared her silky skin, and the expression of total sensual absorption on his face made her nipples tighten even more, her breasts throb for want of his touch, and the secret place at the top of her thighs swell and grow wet. She whispered his name.

Craig looked at her then, really looked at her, and Chelsea finally saw his inner conflict. In spite of how he'd treated her, she realized that he still cared, even if he hadn't wanted her to know the truth, even if he'd steadfastly refused to admit it, and even if he denied it later. Her heart nearly bursting with renewed hope and fledgling trust, she allowed the last self-protective barrier circling her emotions to tumble free.

SEVEN

Releasing his hold on her loosely bound wrists, Craig brought his hands to Chelsea's breasts and lightly fingered her taut nipples. She moaned, the pleading sound that escaped her an eloquent statement of need.

"Talk to me," Craig muttered as he leaned down. After skimming the side of her neck with his lips, he retraced his path with the tip of his tongue while simultaneously plucking at her nipples. "Tell me what you want."

She spoke softly, and from her heart. "I want you to make love to me."

His facial features settled into defensive lines, and he said, "We're having sex."

She shook her head, denial automatic. "No, Craig, we're not."

He silenced her with a quick, hard kiss, then dropped to his knees and cupped the weight of her full breasts in his hands. He hesitated for a moment before he met her gaze. "I can't promise you anything, Chelsea. All I can tell you is that we'll use each other, and it will probably be the most honest thing we ever share."

Her expression gentle, she said, "I'm not asking for promises, just the tenderness I remember."

She thought she glimpsed regret in his eyes before he looked away. She heard his ragged sigh and hoped that he might say something more, but he didn't. He licked her nipples then, his tongue abrading her sensitive flesh with tantalizing swipes and teasing jabs. He alternated back and forth until she felt swollen and achy with need.

Chelsea struggled free of the shirt caught at her wrists and let it drift to the floor. She gripped Craig's shoulders in order to remain standing. He seemed oblivious to her weak-kneed condition as he pursued a course of erotic torture that left her quivering. Her hunger for him raced through her body with reckless abandon.

He touched her everywhere. He sipped at her nipples like a parched man, then painted her belly with wet, hot caresses that eventually turned into stinging kisses. She felt the tremors that shook his hands as they roamed over the curves and hollows of her body, and she sensed that Craig needed her in ways that exceeded physical desire.

His fingers slid between her knees, his knuckles sending chill bumps across her skin when he dragged them up and down her inner thighs. She willingly parted her legs, her cooperation aiding him as he slipped her panties over her hips and down her legs, where they pooled briefly at her ankles before she kicked aside the scrap of white silk.

Chelsea welcomed his intimate foray when he cupped her, curving his palm over her tight auburn curls with a possessiveness that nearly shattered her. Trembling, she whispered his name over and over again in a feverish sounding chant, then gasped when he tucked two narrow fingers into the heart of her desire.

As he probed and fondled her, he sucked her nipples more forcefully, alternating between her breasts until she feared she might go insane. Chelsea drove her fingers into his long dark hair, bracketing his head between her palms as he worked his magic on her. She tried to catch her breath, but she failed. Sensation after sensation rocked her as he dipped his narrow fingers into and out of the snug, humid recess.

Craig stopped abruptly and withdrew his hand. Chelsea moaned, the loss of his touch devastating, but she sighed with relief just seconds later when he sank into a low crouch and positioned one of her legs over his shoulder. Recalling the uniquely erotic ritual from years past, she understood and welcomed his intent. She felt wanton as her heart raced and her pulse points hammered like drums.

Chelsea straightened, pressing her back against the wall. Her breathing swift and shallow, she felt Craig's warm breath wash across her most sensitive flesh a heartbeat before his mouth settled over her. She shivered uncontrollably, the shock to her body undeniable.

She groaned when she felt the first boldly intimate strokes of Craig's tongue. He sucked her, sending every nerve in her body into glittering shock. Flicking his tongue back and forth across the swollen nub no longer concealed from view, Craig tantalized and tortured her even as he stroked the delicate skin of her inner thighs with his fingertips.

She felt faint. She felt incendiary. And she felt ready to die from the pleasure he heaped on her. With only one clear thought dominating her mind, she frantically tugged at Craig's shoulders. She wanted him naked and buried deep inside her body, and she was willing to sell her soul if that's what it took to get him there.

As though sensing her desperation, Craig surged to his feet, shrugged out of his unfastened shirt, and reached for the button at the waistband of his jeans. Chelsea's hands were quicker. Breathless with need, she caressed him through the worn fabric, the strength and heat of his aroused flesh almost searing her fingertips.

Her eyes riveted on his strained features, she stroked him with a new boldness and a sense of purpose she credited to years of suppressed hunger and loneliness. She felt utterly greedy and completely without inhibitions.

Craig groaned her name. Chelsea's heart called out to him in response. He shuddered, unable to contain his reaction to her intimate stroking.

She thought he looked like a proud warrior from some primitive culture as he towered over her, his long, still damp hair flowing past his broad shoulders, the gold stud gleaming in his earlobe, and the angular bones of his face giving him such an enigmatic look that his thoughts were impossible to read. He shuddered yet again beneath her fingertips.

"I want more of you," she whispered, her own body throbbing with incredible intensity. "I *need* more of you."

Craig jerked a nod at her. She watched his jaws tighten and felt the muscles in his whole body clench as she freed the button, slowly lowered the zipper, and then shoved his jeans and briefs down past his narrow hips. He sprang free, his arousal pulsing with power. Chelsea clasped him between her hands, the smooth, hot feel of him taking her breath away.

Craig muttered an indecipherable word, the sound a heady blend of unexpressed emotions and physical need. "I can't wait."

Chelsea almost missed his guttural comment. She felt a stunning sense of loss when he stepped back from her and discarded his clothing, but in the next second all her worries disappeared. Craig seized her by the waist, lifted her until their eyes met and locked, and pressed her against the wall. He shifted forward, his muscular body in glorious restraint.

Craig kept her there, pinned against the wall like a sacrifice awaiting his penetration. His arousal throbbed against the welcoming, waiting heat at the top of her thighs. Chelsea circled his torso with her arms and legs. Her breasts plumped against his chest, her nipples nudging into the dense pelt.

"Let me love you, Craig."

His eyes went as black as midnight and his sensual lips whitened with tension. She saw the war he waged with himself in his troubled gaze, the brawl between the man once capable of love and sensitivity and the man who'd learned to hate and who refused to expose his emotions.

"Love me, Craig. Oh dear heaven, please love me."

He speared into her without a single word of warning, burying himself to the hilt. She cried out, in surprise and with heartfelt relief. She felt alive for the first time in six years.

Plunging repeatedly and as deeply into her as he could, Craig gripped her hips, his fingers digging into her skin. Chelsea met each upward thrust with a twisting uptilt of her pelvis. The inner muscles of her body quivered and sucked at him. She peppered his exposed neck with kisses until he claimed her mouth and duplicated with his tongue the frantic motion of his lower body. She reveled in the power of his arousal and the rippling strength of his body as he possessed her.

He ate at her lips, seemingly insatiable and

utterly ruthless in his search for satisfaction, but Chelsea knew in her heart that Craig was still hiding, still shielding himself from the risks inherent in loving. She forgave him his defensive attitude and his bitterness, she abandoned the self-protective instincts that she'd acquired during their years apart, and she surrendered completely, allowing her body to express the emotions she knew Craig would reject if she made the mistake of voicing her feelings.

She loved him with searching kisses and through the intimate joining of their loins. And she tried to help him heal his wounded heart, even though she knew better than to expect too much, too soon from a man as stubborn and vulnerable as Craig Wilder.

They mated without words of love, their passion fierce, very nearly violent as ghosts from their shared past pursued them. Greedy mouths locked together, they slammed against each other, mindless as they sought completion.

Chelsea neared her summit almost before she realized it. She felt poised at the edge of a precipice, the promise of release within her grasp. She inhaled sharply, then stiffened, the coiled tension of her body on the verge of snapping. She clutched at Craig's shoulders, her body beyond her control, her need for release so great that tears flooded her eyes and spilled down her cheeks.

She trembled, unconsciously digging her nails into his shoulders. "Craig?" Even she heard the anxiety in her voice.

"Don't fight it," he said raspily against her lips. He jerked against her, the depth and angle of his penetration a reflection of his sensory memory of Chelsea's needs in the throes of passion. "Let go, little one. Let go."

Sensation imploded deep within her, then shuddered outward to encompass her, consume her, and, she feared in a moment of shocked panic, drown her. She unravelled like a spinning top. Unable to stop herself, Chelsea screamed.

Craig inhaled the sound into his body as he pumped into her, his own quest for completion still driving him. Clinging to him, Chelsea felt her insides shatter into a thousand shards of sensation. He gripped her hips even more tightly, his near-frenzied bucking sending her into a star-studded oblivion that denied her coherence and rewarded her with ecstasy.

In the aftermath of Chelsea's climax, Craig groaned low in his throat. He splintered several moments later, his life force jetting like hot lava into her depths in a lengthy release that nearly sent him to his knees. He felt almost paralyzed as he collapsed against her, flattening her against the wall as he struggled not just for air, but for the strength to lift himself away from her body before he crushed her.

Craig eventually braced his upper body weight with his forearms positioned on either side of Chelsea's head, his breathing still unsteady, his heart hammering wildly in his chest, and his body soaked with sweat. As he began to shift his hips, she rebelled. Her hands gripped his narrow waist in a silent plea that he not withdraw from her.

He remembered then the way they'd held each other once the sensual storms had passed, their bodies replete, their emotions enriched by the intimacies they'd shared. He also remembered their quiet conversations, as well as Chelsea's breathless laughter and his own unceasing need to retest the boundaries of their desire for each other even when they were already limp from the fatigue of hours of lovemaking. Craig felt his anger with Chelsea start to diminish as he drifted in the past, his memories becoming so poignant that he wound up fighting to control his emotions.

Chelsea recovered slowly, her thoughts muzzy and her body atremble with pleasurable aftershocks. When she finally stirred and nuzzled

Craig's neck with her lips, he lifted his bowed head and peered down at her. She returned his curious gaze, the uncertainty in her eyes and the hesitant smile lifting the edges of her generous mouth making him wary again. He studied her in silence. He also readied himself to deal with her regret and the recriminations that might follow.

"I'm glad this happened," she confessed before she undulated against his sturdy body and pressed her lips to the side of his muscular neck. "It was wonderful, more wonderful than all of my memories of us put together."

Shock rippled through him, and he felt as though someone had hit him in the chest with a well-aimed brick. Torn suddenly between shaking her for being so unpredictable and throwing her out into the thunderstorm and letting her fend for herself because she'd become a complication he didn't need, Craig muttered an ugly self-directed phrase that called into question his own mother's character. In the end, though, he bowed to neither impulse. He succumbed instead to more basic needs, needs too long left unappeased.

Easing backward, he cupped Chelsea's chin with his hand and forced her to meet his gaze. He felt his body harden with a renewed onslaught of desire as he tried to read and understand the dreamy look in her eyes. Although he resented her ability to seduce him with just a look, Craig didn't try to disengage their bodies. He took her mouth, angry with his inability to deny himself the pleasure she offered as he hungrily slanted his lips over hers and delved into her honeyed sweetness.

Seizing her wrists, Craig shackled them above her head with one hand. Chelsea smiled against his lips and arched into him with feline grace. He felt her inner core quiver hotly as he grew inside her, the slick heat of her body searing him, seducing him, and warning him that he wouldn't ever get enough of this woman, no matter how many times he took her.

He claimed her for a second time, claimed what had been his so many years ago. As he surged repeatedly into her, he told himself that she owed him the satisfaction he wanted again, even if it meant using her body until he tired of it and her.

Although he made a valiant effort, Craig failed to reconcile in his own mind the real reasons for her answering passion and sensual generosity. Shuddering violently when Chelsea's tongue darted into his mouth to duel and taunt, he realized that he felt too greedy, and far too needy, to question her motives any longer. He would do that later, he promised himself as his muscular body knotted with erotic tension and devastating sensations swept through him.

"You're better now," Craig admitted as he pushed aside his empty plate and soup bowl.

Chelsea looked up from her half-eaten sandwich. "I was never a bad cook, just not very experienced."

"I'm not talking about food."

Stillness settled over her. "What are you talking about?"

"Sex."

"You once told me that I should always trust my instincts in that department." She forced a smile. "I simply followed your advice."

"Your instincts were excellent a little while ago."

She heard the grudging tone in his voice and deliberately leaned back in her chair, the thrust of her breasts apparent beneath her shirt. She felt Craig's gaze follow her as she shifted, provocation inherent in the less than subtle movement of her upper torso. Her unrestrained breasts swayed gently, the material chafing her already sensitive nipples. "Thank you. I'm glad you approve. I guess that means I didn't disappoint you."

"I didn't say that," he ground out, his gaze lingering on her breasts. She lifted her arms, stretched, and then slowly lowered her hands to her lap.

She gave him an innocent look when their eyes finally met, even though they both knew she hadn't fooled him into thinking her behavior was anything but intentional. "But you meant to," she remarked with more confidence than she actually felt. "Didn't you?"

Craig shrugged and abruptly changed the subject. "The storm's starting to let up, but you'll have to stay for a few days. Things have to dry out before there'll be a safe way to get you out of here."

She nodded, secretly pleased that Mother Nature had given her the time she needed with Craig. "I don't mind. Do you?"

He frowned, as though the sound of her soft voice grated on his nerves. "It makes no difference to me."

"Good. I noticed that you left our clothes on the shower floor. Do you mind if I do a load of laundry?" Chelsea reached for her iced tea, dipped a finger into the glass, and made the cubes bob and rattle. "Those mud stains are going to be a nightmare to get out if I don't do something about them fairly soon." Removing her wet finger from the glass, she sucked the tip dry, her eyes on his face the entire time.

Stop thinking about the past, she ordered silently. *Think about me and the future. Give me a chance to help you see the possibilities ahead of us, because they're limitless.*

Sounding disconcerted, Craig demanded, "What the hell are you up to?"

"Just trying to rescue my sweater and slacks from the rag pile and be a good guest."

"You're not a guest. You're my ex-wife."

"True, but you don't need to make my legal status sound like a fate worse than death."

"I don't trust you, Chelsea. I never will."

She felt the sting of his words. "You've already made your feelings about me very clear. Since I'm neither deaf nor blind, I've gotten your message, but I still think your attitude is your problem, not mine."

Craig shoved himself to his feet, the legs of his chair scraping angrily across the wooden floor. Leaning down, he planted his big hands on the table. "Be careful, *babe*. You're in way over your head here."

She gave him a serene look, flexing rusty

feminine wiles when she said, "You're tense again. I think you need me to help you relax."

Chelsea suppressed her laughter when she saw his stunned expression. She liked surprising Craig, especially since she resented his apparent need to classify her as a species that ranked somewhere beneath an earthworm. He moved with the speed of lightning.

Instinctively certain that he had no intention of harming her, Chelsea let him jerk her to her feet and slam her against his chest. Plastered against his hard body like a fresh coat of paint, she grinned up at him. "You do want me, don't you?"

He replied by bracketing her hips between his hands. He pulled her up and against his loins, positioning her so she felt every throbbing inch of his arousal through his jeans. "Damn you," he said, his low, intense voice sending a shiver up her spine.

Even though his words almost sounded like a caress, Chelsea didn't kid herself. She understood Craig's meaning. Regret saturated her emotions and made her heart ache for him. Trailing her fingertips across his lips, she pressed her palm to his cheek. "Don't damn me. Make love to me instead. I know it's what we both want."

"You're a witch."

He made the accusation in such a halfhearted way that Chelsea almost smiled. She tried to lighten his mood. "Shall I cast a spell?" she asked, laughter suddenly bursting to life inside her and bubbling free before she could stop it. She realized then that she was happier with Craig, even a defensive and unpredictable Craig, than she'd been in years.

"You already have," he muttered, sounding tense and irritable again.

"Please let go of your anger. If you don't, it'll eat you alive."

"I can't," he muttered, a fleeting glimmer of unacknowledged pain and then his fear of betrayal reflected in his troubled gaze as he studied her face. "And I won't. It's what kept me alive."

She wondered if he understood just how revealing his admission was, especially since she'd learned, too, that anger could be a powerful motivating force. Chelsea felt tears sting her eyes, but she blinked them away. She didn't want Craig ever to think she pitied him, even though it killed her that he'd been betrayed and humiliated by a legal system he'd once championed. "You don't need to protect yourself from me. I wouldn't ever do anything to hurt you."

He stiffened. "You don't have that kind of power over me any longer."

Patience, she reminded herself. He needed every shred of patience she possessed. "This isn't about power, Craig. This is only about the two of us and the choices we make while we're together."

Chelsea paused, searching his features for some sign that he might be willing to let down some of his defenses. Unfortunately, she saw nothing to encourage her, but she still refused to give up. Before he could stop her, she slid her arms around his neck, tugged his head down, and enveloped his lips in a hot, openmouthed kiss meant to scorch his soul.

Craig took her peace offering, despite a moment of hesitation that didn't surprise Chelsea at all. He sampled every bit of her, his hunger seemingly endless as he ate at her lips and used his tongue like a marauding warrior on the inside of her mouth. He even kept their lips joined when he lifted her into his arms, hauled her across the room, and settled her onto the oval rug in front of the fireplace. Kneeling between her parted legs, he grabbed the tails of her shirt.

Chelsea stayed his hands with a gentle touch. "I'm going to be sewing buttons for the rest of my life if you keep this up, and you're going to run out of clothes if you aren't careful."

His knuckles whitened. "Then get rid of the shirt."

"Help me," she invited, wanting him with an intensity that made her voice shake. "I'll start at the top, and you start at the bottom. We'll meet in the middle."

They did, and the process took less than five seconds.

Craig flipped open the front panels of the shirt, his hands fisting in the fabric as his heated gaze skimmed her nakedness. "You're skin has always reminded me of the finest porcelain, but it's never cold to the touch." He reached up and brushed her nipples with his fingertips, then watched them bead into tight coral knots. A muscle ticked high in his cheek.

She stared at him, shocked by his comment. She also trembled, her body sending a silent but profound message of desire. His expression intent, Craig rolled her nipples between his fingers, then gently plucked at them until Chelsea moaned.

His gaze drifted down her torso to her silky auburn curls. His fingers followed his eyes, slowly moving over her skin, lingering here, tantalizing there. Chelsea held her breath when he curved his hand over her mound, his touch possessive as he stared at her and silently challenged her to deny him what he desired.

She let out a lusty sigh. Sensation after sensation sang over her skin and spiraled into her bloodstream as he combed his fingers through the auburn veil. "No one's touched me since you went away," she whispered, praying he would believe the truth, but also fearful that she might have spoken too soon.

Craig paused, his gaze so sharp and so filled with suspicion that she felt wounded. He took his time evaluating her sincerity. Chelsea knew the instant he judged her a liar, but she didn't bother to plead her case.

Cradling her hips with his hands, Craig leaned forward and used his lips and tongue to leave darting trails of fire along the sleek line of her belly and over the gentle rise of each hipbone. His hair swept over her skin like a caress.

Chelsea fingered strands of his long hair, then drove her fingers into the depths of the dark mane as he moved to her breasts and sucked. She trembled beneath his skilled mouth, her hands falling weakly to her sides. She could scarcely catch her breath.

Craig straightened. Chelsea remained silent

and still under his intent gaze, and her love for him helped her find the patience she needed to deal with her ex-husband's complex nature and skeptical attitude.

"No one should have a body like yours," he finally remarked.

"Why not?" she whispered.

"You're a walking temptation."

She smiled, unable to stop herself. "I couldn't walk right now if my life depended on it, but are you tempted anyway?"

He brought his hands to her belly, his palms hot as he splayed his fingers over her in a possessive gesture that spoke volumes. "I don't want to be," he admitted.

"I understand," she whispered, saddened by his honesty but not willing to hide from it. She extended her hands. He took them and pulled her up so that they sat knee to knee.

As they faced each other he closed his eyes, rolling his head from side to side while he massaged his neck. Chelsea simply waited and watched him, her body throbbing with hunger. She recognized Craig's need to orchestrate their intimacy, and she felt willing to let him set their pace.

He finally met her gaze as he placed his hands on the insides of her upper thighs. His fingertips nudged against the warm creases of her body. He stroked her, making her swell with tension and moisten in anticipation of an even more intimate intrusion into her body.

"I didn't expect to want you so much," he admitted. "I thought I was past it. I thought I was over you."

She covered his hands with her own, savoring his honesty. "You aren't obligated by anything that happens between us, Craig. Besides, I'm not a fool. I realize what this is all about."

"And what exactly do you think this is about, other than sex?" he demanded sharply.

In order to answer his question, she took a moment to summon her flagging courage. "This is your game, and you're making up the rules as you go along. If I accept your rules and make no demands, I'm welcome to play until you get bored."

"I don't understand you anymore."

Chelsea took little comfort in the amazement she saw in his expression. "You will eventually, but only if you want to."

"You aren't the woman I married eight years ago."

"And you aren't the man I lost six years ago. Does that make us even?" Chelsea asked. "Or does that simply mean we have to adjust to the changes in each other if we want to spend time together?"

"You're oversimplifying."

She took one of his hands and lifted it to her breast. "This is the only thing between us that's simple. You want me, and I want you."

"As you just said, I'm using you." He kneaded her flesh, his sensual touch making a mockery of his blunt words even if he didn't seem to realize it.

Chelsea felt like putty beneath his hands. She wanted to groan and fling herself into his arms, but she stayed still and remained focused on his train of thought. "I know, but isn't that how your world works? People use each other, and only the strong survive."

"I'm surprised."

"Don't be. I lived in your world since you went away. It's a far cry from the one we once shared, and I may hate it, but it's reality."

"We were fools. We deluded ourselves into thinking we could escape the dark side of life."

Chelsea quickly disagreed. "No, we were in love."

"Illusions won't get you through life. Love won't, either."

"But neither will your bitterness, Craig.

You're using it to protect yourself, and it's blinding you to the good side of life."

He exhaled harshly. "I don't want to talk anymore."

"Then we won't talk," Chelsea said softly. She leaned forward, already reaching for the zipper of his jeans as she nipped at his chin with gentle teeth.

Craig broke free of her, surged to his feet, and stripped down to the skin. Resuming his place on the rug, he brought Chelsea's hands to his pulsing arousal. She whispered kisses over his face and stroked his hard length, silently marveling over the satin feel of his sex and the realization that his strength would soon be submerged within the depths of her body. He slid his fingers up her inner thighs to explore the silk-covered heat of her desire, and he claimed her mouth in such a way that she felt cherished for the first time in years.

Chelsea and Craig communicated without words after that, their desire eclipsing the realities that still haunted them. Their journey to satisfaction was a timeless and intensely erotic interlude that set in motion a subtle redefinition of their relationship.

EIGHT

The storm finally ended late that afternoon. A warming trend, replete with bright sunshine and gentle breezes, settled over the area the next morning. The threat of additional flash floods disappeared as nature undertook the process of recovery and renewal in the days that followed. Birds resumed their nest building, the standing pools of water started to evaporate, errant streams dried up, and a family of raccoons cavorted at the edge of the clearing.

Chelsea and Craig settled into their own routine. However awkward and tentative their attempt at coexistence, Chelsea didn't question her good fortune or Craig's motives.

He disappeared early each morning, devoting long hours to rebuilding the bridge over the ravine. Using his Jeep and a flatbed trailer, he transported timber that had been stored in the shed behind the cabin, as well as tools and rope.

When questioned by Chelsea, Craig explained that he intended to span the ravine with the several lengths of sturdy timber and bolt them to the frame of the old bridge, which had survived the storm. If he succeeded, he told her, he would be able to drive her to her car.

She offered to help, but Craig declined so abruptly that she didn't mention the subject again. She remained unaware of the alternate overland route available to them, as well as Craig's rationale that the bridge needed to be repaired anyway.

Chelsea stayed at the cabin. She relaxed, sampled a few of the paperback books Craig kept in his bookcase, napped, and took periodic walks to stretch her legs during his absences. The bruises on her back and hips grew colorful, but she quickly recovered from the residual aches and pains caused by her fall into the ravine.

She saw Craig's exhaustion following the long hours he spent working on the bridge repairs, and she encouraged him to slow his pace. She didn't admit how unenthusiastic she felt about leaving Craig or his isolated cabin or her hope that his reconstruction project would take more time than he expected.

She stayed busy, utilizing the contents of the pantry and freezer to create inviting meals. Craig said little about the food she prepared, but he invariably cleaned his plate and then asked for a second, and sometimes a third, helping. If he found her culinary skills unexpected, he didn't comment.

He frequently lapsed into protracted silences when they were together in the evenings, but Chelsea kept her own counsel and didn't press him for explanations about his thoughts or feelings. She went eagerly into his arms. She caught periodic glimpses of the gentle man she'd once known during those breathlessly vulnerable moments that followed their often tempestuous lovemaking, but for the most part he remained aloof and watchful whenever they were together.

Even though they made love frequently, Craig's obvious aversion to sleeping together at night bothered Chelsea more than she wanted to admit. She assumed that he felt determined to avoid any real emotional closeness. During their fifth evening together, she dared voice her curiosity about his attitude—but only after they'd made love.

"Why won't you let me come to bed with you at night?"

He finished zipping his jeans before he looked at her. "I sleep alone, Chelsea, and my reasons are personal."

"We used to do some of our best talking late at night," she reminded him softly.

"There's nothing to talk about."

She suppressed her frustration, but his rejection still hurt. She also reminded herself for the tenth time that day that she courted disappointment if she expected anything other than a sexual relationship with Craig. Tugging her blanket over her naked body, she watched him from her reclining position on the couch.

As was his nightly habit, Craig sat on the floor in front of the fireplace and stared at the flickering flames. He leaned forward, his fingertips going to his forehead. As he bowed his head and massaged his temples, his long hair drifted forward to obscure his profile.

Chelsea quelled the urge to join him and offer comfort. Her gaze shifted to the network of scars on his lower back and lingered there. She still hadn't found the nerve to ask him what had produced them.

As though sensing her thoughts, Craig twisted suddenly, his eyes filled with hostility. Chelsea froze, embarrassed to have been caught staring.

He surged to his feet. She saw his tension not only in the stark expression on his face, but also in the rippling muscles of his powerful body as he walked out of the room and down the hallway to his bedroom.

Chelsea exhaled shakily, the feelings of contentment she'd found in his embrace only a short while ago disappearing. She silently mourned his constant defensiveness, not just the sense of helplessness it provoked within her.

Feeling sad and defeated, Chelsea huddled beneath her blanket and fought the tears stinging her eyes. She eventually fell asleep in her solitary bed, but she jerked awake a few hours later when she heard Craig shouting from the back bedroom. Gathering the blanket around her naked body, Chelsea ran to his open bedroom door. She paused, uncertainty filling her.

Moonlight spilled across his naked body. She watched him toss and turn in his sleep, and she longed to chase away the demons that tortured him. Still, she waited. He stiffened suddenly, his body turning as rigid as a slab of stone. Shouting a curse just seconds later, he began to thrash around again.

Alarmed, Chelsea moved soundlessly across the floor on bare feet. She reached out, her fingers curving gently over Craig's shoulder as she stood at the side of his bed. His name died unvoiced when hands came out of nowhere, jerked her off her feet, and tumbled her onto the bed. She lost the blanket as she sailed through the air and landed facedown on the mattress.

She fought to free herself from the hand that shackled her wrists together behind her back, but she failed. With her heart in her throat, she felt a second hand fist in her long hair and yank her head up.

"Craig!" she screamed once she caught her breath. She felt more frightened than she'd ever been in her life. "Please stop. You're hurting me."

He stiffened, released her, and flipped her onto her back. Straddling her hips, Craig grabbed her hands, pinned them above her head, and leaned over her, his expression threatening as air heaved in and out of his body. Shocked, Chelsea stared up at him, afraid to move, afraid to do anything.

"What the hell are you trying to do?"

"Nothing, I swear. What's wrong?" she whispered. "What did I do?"

"Answer my question."

"I heard you shouting in your sleep. I was worried about you," she explained, still trembling from the shock of being treated like a criminal.

"I dream," he said through gritted teeth.

Chelsea saw what the admission cost him. "I know."

"How the hell do you know?"

She swallowed to clear away the cottony feeling in her throat. "I heard you last night after you went to bed. And the night before."

Craig released her hands and straightened, his weight settling on her upper thighs, the muscles of his body still rippling with tension. He drove his fingers into his long hair, covering his eyes with the heels of his hands. Chelsea rubbed her wrists, her gaze locked on the portion of his face that she could still see, which in the moonlight seemed even more etched with strain than usual.

"Is this why you won't let me sleep with you?"

He lowered his hands and met her gaze. "I'm liable to kill you, Chelsea, and I don't want that on my conscience."

She placed her hands on his powerful thighs. Muscles bunched beneath her palms and fingers, and his coarse body hair made her skin tingle. "I'm sorry. I really didn't understand the risk involved."

"Don't come anywhere near me when I'm sleeping."

She nodded. "All right."

"I mean it. If you need me for something, call out from the doorway."

"This is one of the reasons you're determined to stay out here alone, isn't it?"

He ignored her question at first, climbed off of her, and stretched out on his back, his hands tucked beneath his head. Several silent minutes passed before he said. "I'm not fit to be around decent people."

"That's not true, and you know it," Chelsea insisted. She took his hand and loosely wove their fingers together. "I wish you'd told me. Is there anything I can do to help?"

"It's not your responsibility."

She moved cautiously into a seated position beside his hip, her naked body the epitome of unconscious grace rather than deliberate provocation as she sat in a pool of moonlight. Her skin appeared as pale as fresh cream, and the expression on her face remained gentle.

"Craig, we aren't talking about responsibility right now. We're talking about simple compassion. I don't expect anything in return."

"You cannot change what I've become, so forget it."

"Let me help you," she pleaded as she gripped his hand. "It's killing me to see you so tied up in knots all the time." The tears brimming in her eyes spilled free, splashing their joined hands. "Please, let me help."

He drew her forward. Relief filled her when he pulled her down beside him. Placing her hand over Craig's heart, she pressed her cheek to his shoulder. Chelsea felt a shudder rumble through him, and then another. She sighed with relief when he circled her shoulders with his arm and brought her even closer.

"Did I tell you yet about my job?" she asked, determined to distract him, if only for a short while, from his dark thoughts and painful memories.

"You hardly need to work."

"That's not the point."

"What is the point?"

"Knowing that my time is well spent, which it is in the child custody division of family court."

"I take it you dusted off your court reporter

certificate," he commented. "Which judge are you working for?"

"Mary Templeton."

"She's good."

"I've always admired her, but seeing her work with the young people who've become a point of contention between divorcing parents is amazing. I asked to be assigned to her after I saw her handle a particularly difficult case involving a little girl with leukemia. The parents were so wrapped up in their own battle, they couldn't see what they were doing to their sick daughter. Mary got their attention before it was too late, and the little girl is in remission now."

"You always liked children," he remarked, his voice subdued.

I loved our baby, she said in the silence of her mind. *I loved him with all my heart even though I lost him.* Chelsea forced her thoughts past the pregnancy that had ended in a miscarriage during Craig's prosecution, the baby he knew nothing about, the baby she still mourned.

"Mary's one of those judges who seems to have the wisdom of Solomon when determining what's best for the children who visit her in chambers," Chelsea continued. "She helped me when Dad was dying. She also pitched in while

I was settling his estate. We've become good friends despite the difference in our ages." Although Chelsea felt Craig stiffen when she mentioned her father, she knew they couldn't avoid the subject forever.

"How did he die?" he finally asked.

"Liver cancer. He had a pretty rough time of it."

"If you're looking for sympathy for the old man, I haven't got any to waste on him."

"I don't expect that of you. I know what kind of a man he was, Craig. I had to deal with him after you were sent to prison, and I took care of him when he became ill. It was a difficult situation, especially when he insisted on being cared for at home."

"Why didn't you hire a nurse?"

"I did. Seven in the space of three months. He made their lives a living hell. Nurse number eight lasted until the end only because he'd slipped into a coma."

"You idolized him. Watching him die couldn't have been easy on you."

Surprised by his compassion, she agreed, "It wasn't easy, but not because I idolized him. The truth is that I was afraid of his disapproval, and I wasted a lot of years trying to earn his respect. It took his death to make me understand that the only approval I require is my own."

"He was a sorry son of a—"

Chelsea pressed her fingers against his lips. "Please listen to me. I really believe that God punished him with a lingering and painful death because of what he did to you, so don't waste your time or your energy on him anymore. He's gone, and he can't harm either one of us ever again."

Craig took her hand, pressed a kiss into the center of her palm, and then said, "My common sense tells me you're right, but my gut still wants vengeance."

"I don't know what else to say to you, except to remind you again that he's dead and your only real vindication will come through the courts."

Chelsea felt the steady rhythm of his heartbeat beneath her palm. Curling against Craig, she gave him time to gather his thoughts.

"You're more forgiving than I'll ever be, but then you have less to forgive, don't you?"

"That's a matter of opinion," she reminded him as she recalled the lies her father had told her about Craig during his prosecution.

"What else do you do with your time?" he asked.

She leaned up and pressed a kiss on his chin,

proud of him for making an effort to control his anger. "I take one day at a time, just like most people."

He glanced down at her, studying her expression intently. "You wanted to talk. Remember?"

Chelsea grinned. "I remember. I'm doing volunteer work at St. Mary's. They have a new pediatric cancer wing."

His surprise obvious, he whistled. "Tough work keeping a positive attitude. Why put yourself through the stress?"

"The children are remarkable. I've learned a lot about courage from them."

"You're different in many ways now, aren't you?"

"I was so immature before, but now . . . now I'm more realistic."

Craig shifted suddenly, rolling onto his side so that they faced each other. Chelsea felt his hand settle on her hip, then the press of his fingertips as he urged her closer. She shimmied forward, arching into him so that her breasts plumped against his hard chest. Slipping her arms around his shoulders, she shifted her pelvis to an intimate position against his loins.

Craig's entire body responded, a ripple of tension passing through him, then a shudder before he thrust his hips against hers. "You were trying to provoke me with all those stories about other men."

"Are you asking me or telling me?"

"Telling."

She nodded, relief sweeping through her. "I was trying to provoke you, but only because you insisted on judging me so harshly."

"And you told me the truth when you said no one had touched you since I've been gone."

"I've never lied to you in my entire life, Craig Wilder, and I don't intend to start now. Too much is at stake."

"Why, Chelsea? We're divorced. You had every right to start a new life."

Her heart sank. *Why*, she wondered, *can't you see how deeply I love you, and how deeply I will always love you?* "I wasn't in the market for a husband." *I had one*, she remembered, *and I want him back.*

"Chelsea . . ."

She swallowed a sob, then whispered, "I didn't want anyone else."

Craig stopped breathing for a long minute and simply looked at her. Chelsea sensed how fragile his trust was, and she didn't press him. She sighed with relief when he gently tucked her face into the muscular curve between his shoulder and neck. He held her then, absorbing the trembling of her slender body as he offered her the security of his embrace. She'd missed being held. She'd missed feeling safe and loved. She'd missed quiet talks in the dark of their bedroom. And she'd missed him, her husband, her lover, and her best friend.

"I believe you, Chelsea."

"Then we're making progress."

"I wanted to think the worst of you," he confessed. "It made hating you easier."

"I may have been a failure as a wife, but I'm not a liar."

"You weren't a failure."

"You don't have to defend me. The simple truth is that I wasn't there for you when you needed me. I couldn't be."

"I suspect we have your father to thank for that." His hold on her tightened. "Damn the man! He shouldn't have been able to rob me of everything and everyone I valued."

"I wish my father had been a better person. Our lives would have been quite different now."

Craig rolled onto his back without warning. He took Chelsea with him, lifting her effortlessly. She wound up astride his powerful loins, her knees bent and her lower legs pressed against his thighs. She leaned forward, her hands coming to rest on either side of his head, her hair an exotic frame to her delicate features, and her breasts swaying against his chest. "What are you thinking?" she asked.

As if she posed a temptation he felt compelled to resist for the moment, Craig lifted her away from his chest. "I still don't understand why you came here."

"The journal," she reminded him. "You need it."

"The postal system works, however inefficiently at times."

"When I found it among his papers and books, I didn't stop to think. I just knew you deserved to have it. I think I made the right decision, even if I made it in haste."

Craig spanned her waist with his hands, his body responding with heat and hardness to their intimate alignment. Chelsea slid across him like syrup, her breasts meeting the hard wall of his chest as she brought her legs together and locked his pulsing arousal between her upper thighs.

"No other reason?" he muttered roughly, his hands bracketing her hips in order to still the less than subtle rocking motion of her lower body.

"I care about you. I've never stopped caring."

"I don't want to believe you."

"That's your choice," she said, her lips so close to his mouth that she inhaled his breath when he exhaled.

"I'm not any good for you or anyone else. Hell, I can't even get through the night yet."

"Because of your memories of prison?"

He nodded, his expression grim.

"Someone once told me that good memories can be used to fight off the bad ones." She paused, aware that she risked his displeasure if she continued. "Maybe your nightmares wouldn't be so bad if you told me about your life in prison."

"There's nothing to say."

"Of course there is. For instance, how did you spend your days?"

"I passed the time."

"You're being difficult," she chided as she rested her head on his shoulder and slipped her arms around his neck.

"All right, Chelsea. I'll play your game, but only up to a point. What do you want to know?"

"Anything you want to tell me."

"I got up at six, washed my face, brushed my teeth, and then I waited to be let out of my cage."

"You were in an individual cell?"

"Most of the time."

"What happened after breakfast?"

"I went to my job."

"Which was?"

"Working in the library."

"What else did you do?"

"I wrote appeals for inmates who couldn't find representation they trusted."

"You practiced law?"

His voice sounded tighter than an overwound watch as he reminded her, "I was disbarred, Chelsea."

"But you used your legal talent to help others," she clarified softly. "Why?"

"I used my skills to stay alive. They bought me protection, membership in the most powerful segment of the prison population, and a spot on the inmate council."

"But you still had to be on guard twenty-four hours a day, and you couldn't trust anyone."

"Precisely."

"The tension must have been awful for you."

"I adjusted."

"When did you work out?"

Craig frowned. "Every afternoon. Why?"

She lifted her head and smiled at him. "I like the results."

"I'm glad," he muttered gruffly.

She slid her hand the length of his powerful chest, over the ridge of muscles that covered his belly, and down across his lean hip. "I like it a lot." Slipping her hand around his side, Chelsea smoothed her fingers over the puckered flesh she'd seen earlier. When Craig flinched, she asked, "What happened to your back?"

"A knife fight."

"Someone attacked you? With a knife?" Horrified to hear confirmation of what she'd suspected since first spotting the scars, she took a deep breath to steady herself. "Where were the guards?"

"There were two someones, and knives are easy to fashion from silverware or a piece of metal from a bedframe. The guards generally stayed clear of the showers."

"Why did it happen?"

"Why do you think?"

An image flashed in her mind, and she felt instantly ill. "You've been through so much."

"They failed, Chelsea. I made certain they always failed, and the threat ended the day I walked through the front gates," Craig reminded her.

"The threat hasn't ended if you're still having nightmares."

"They'll stop eventually."

"But, Craig . . ."

He shifted her off his body and turned away from her. Stretched out on his side, he faced the wall. "Change the subject. I can't talk about this anymore."

She knelt behind him. "Roll onto your stomach for me."

"Why?"

"Please trust me," she whispered, her fingertips already skimming over his broad shoulders.

Craig cooperated, but Chelsea knew it was only because she posed no real physical threat to him. She gently massaged his back. Working her fingertips over his knotted muscles, she felt the tension in him start to ease.

Craig finally relaxed beneath her hands, and his breathing deepened as she made her way down the entire length of his naked body. She eventually reversed course, moving back up his body at a soothingly steady pace until she reached his narrow waist.

Chelsea paused when she encountered the network of scars on his lower back. She hesitated for a long moment, considered the consequences of what she was about to do, and then leaned forward. She pressed her lips to the damaged skin, hot tears seeping involuntarily from her eyes as she tried in her own way to heal him with her love.

Craig turned on her like an animal pouncing on its prey. Flat on her back in the space of a heartbeat, she stared up at him as he came down over her body.

"What are you trying to do to me?" Craig demanded roughly.

Chelsea swallowed her tears. "I just wanted to give you new memories to replace the bad ones."

"Don't bother. They always fade."

"All of them?"

"All of them, Chelsea."

She nodded to cover her disappointment. "I think I understand what you're saying. It hurts too much to remember, so you shove all the special memories out of your mind until one day they disappear forever." She tried to smile, but she failed to produce much more than a grimace before she admitted, "I couldn't stand being around people who were in love after you went away. I resented their happiness so much that I stopped going out altogether. I shut myself up in our home. I stopped living, and I tried my best to stop feeling."

"Why?" he asked, sounding genuinely baffled. "You're a very social creature. You enjoy people, and people like you."

Chelsea hesitated. She knew the price for her honesty would be high if Craig doubted her sincerity.

"Tell me," he ordered, his hips settling forcefully between her thighs as he braced his upper body weight on his elbows and peered down at her in the semidark room.

"It hurt too much to be reminded of what we'd lost," she said, fighting a fresh onslaught of tears. "I missed you so terribly."

Craig stiffened as though struck by a clenched fist. "I don't understand why you're putting yourself through all this. You didn't have to come here, and you don't have to play true confession with me. I've never asked for, nor have I ever expected, anything like this from you."

"But I need for you to understand."

"What I understand is that I'm pure hell to be around!" he shouted. "I feel and behave like a caged animal most of the time, and I can't seem to stop myself. You're wasting your time, because I'm just using you."

She shook her head. "You still deserve a second chance. I want to help you have it."

"Despite the cost to yourself?"

"That's right."

"You're assuming the role of a sacrificial lamb without any expectations?" he pressed, his skepticism obvious. "I don't believe this. Everyone has an agenda, even you."

"Quit looking for motives where they don't exist," she begged. "Look, I already know that my expectations, fantasies actually, aren't rational, and I don't intend to inflict them on you, so you can stop worrying that I'll ever ask anything of you in return, because I won't."

"What the hell are you talking about now?"

"I'm talking about the fact that I know you'll never love me again," she flared, her emotions in such turmoil that she couldn't control her tongue. "I may have been naive and used poor judgment where you were concerned, but I'm not stupid!"

He held her head between his big hands. "Shut up, Chelsea. I don't want to hear this."

"If I can't talk to you, then who am I supposed to talk to? No one else understands what happened to us, and you're the only person I even halfway trust with my feelings." Chelsea paused to catch her breath. Although still agitated, she intended to be honest, regardless of the cost to her emotions. "You're the only person who ever loved me without a motive, so you tell me who I'm supposed to talk to, Craig Wilder. You tell me, dammit!"

"Why can't you accept reality? I can't be what you need me to be. I just can't."

She opened her mouth to disagree, but Craig cupped her breasts, leaned down, and licked the tips until they hardened into tightly puckered knots of pure sensation. She arched beneath his mouth and hands, her body writhing, pleading for more, her throat paralyzed for the moment. When he stopped sucking her sensitive flesh, she felt bereft and breathless and clung to his shoulders.

"That's all I can offer you," he told her harshly. "I don't have anything else to give."

"It's enough for now. I swear it's enough."

"You'll be leaving here in another day or so," Craig warned. "And you won't be coming back."

"I don't care. Make love to me now. Give me what you can, and I'll find a way to live with it."

"Chelsea." He groaned as he bowed his head, his hair draping their faces. "Don't do this to yourself. Don't let me use you and then throw you away."

Despite his cautionary words, Craig refused to deny her when she tugged his head down and stroked the seam of his lips with the tip of her tongue. His constant hunger for her exploded yet again. Chelsea surrendered totally to the inferno that followed.

NINE

Craig felt a tremor of shock ripple through Chelsea's body when he seized her shoulders and swooped down to claim her lips with a hard, grinding kiss. Slanting his mouth over hers, he thrust his tongue into the moist cavern that awaited him, his assault on her a single-minded sensual rampage. He probed the curves and hollows of her mouth, his tongue rasping, darting, and scavenging as it boldly swept over her warm, wet flesh and smooth teeth.

He inhaled her essence. He ate at her lips, and he greedily drank of her sweetness. He touched her everywhere, his hands shaking and growing rough as they charted her nakedness.

He branded her for all eternity, putting his mark of possession on her with a thoroughness that made a lie out of his earlier remark that he had nothing left to offer her. Clinging to her declaration that she had no expectations of him, he felt free to offer what little he possessed, and that little was his soul.

She matched him touch for touch, stroke for stroke. Her tongue probed with equal intrusiveness as she scoured his mouth. Feeling the frantic sweep of her hands over his neck and shoulders, Craig wanted to shout his pleasure to the heavens and then announce to anyone who would listen that she was his again. He didn't, though, because he couldn't bear the thought of separating their mouths for even an instant.

He experienced the perfection of her feminine shape when he settled his loins into the cradling welcome of her parted thighs. He exhaled raggedly as she wrapped her legs around his hips and teased his aroused flesh with the seductive rocking motion of her pelvis. He felt ready to burst, but he fought for and found the strength to contain himself.

He savored the feel of her taut-nippled breasts and smooth belly as Chelsea twisted sensuously in his arms and then molded herself to him. Moaning into her mouth as he fed on her, his hunger for her spiked to fever pitch, and his body shuddered and pulsed with a kind of sensual volatility that he doubted he could contain much longer.

Craig gave himself over to the greed Chelsea inspired, his hold on her possessive as they rolled across the bed, legs tangled, arms clinging, torsos blending, and mouths joined. Ceaselessly tasting, touching, stroking, their passion became a frenzied erotic ballet that knew no boundaries.

Craig soon had only one clear thought. He needed to be inside her, needed to sink into her hot depths and lose himself in the mind-shattering sensations her innate sensuality invariably provoked. Only when they'd been joined in the ultimate intimacy had he willingly relinquished his constant rage with situations he couldn't alter and emotions he couldn't control. It was the only time when he felt like a man capable of controlling his own destiny.

Somehow, he realized despite the desire pummeling his senses and threatening his control, Chelsea had become his answer. He knew, though, that he couldn't allow her to sustain that role in his life. She deserved more, a whole man, a man free of bitterness and an appetite for revenge. Craig reminded himself yet again that she was a temporary reprieve, nothing more. He couldn't risk thinking of her as a permanent part of his life, because he already tempted fate, not just his own carnal nature, each time he took her.

Sprawled atop her, Craig suddenly wrenched his mouth free and tried to catch his breath. He threw back his head, the muscles in his neck corded with the strain of self-control. He wanted, needed her now, but her petite body prompted him to put the brakes on his desire. Granted, she was like a wildcat when aroused, but he still feared his ability to harm her physically if he lost total control.

He felt her hands at his shoulders. Her fingers kneaded his muscular flesh, her frustration evident as her nails scored his skin. He barely felt the pain when he heard his name spill breathlessly from her lips, the bewilderment in the sound touching his heart.

"Trust me, little one," he urged. "Trust me."

She quieted instantly, her response to his whispered words humbling. He suddenly grasped the power she'd allowed him to have over her. Craig shifted onto his side, brought himself up on one elbow, and leaned over her. He captured a nipple between his lips, teething it with a tenderness that concealed the physical tension storming through his entire body.

She said his name again, but this time he

heard wonder and relief. Chelsea reached for him, her palms sliding across his cheeks, her fingers fanning out into his hairline as she urged him closer.

He sucked more forcefully, taking her deeply into his mouth until she whimpered. His other hand strayed down her body and over her quivering belly. She stirred restlessly, her legs parting as he eased his fingers down.

He lightly stroked her cleft, then probed farther to explore the moist, swollen folds of her body. She gasped as he caressed her, inspiring him to tantalize her with every skill he possessed. Craig curved his hand over her, dipping into her with two fingers, testing her readiness and rediscovering in the process the sultriness of her feminine core. He felt her tremble before her hips jerked up from the mattress and forced his fingers more deeply into her tense, simmering center. He immediately felt a corresponding coil of tension tighten to the point of snapping in the depths of his own body.

"Please, Craig," she begged as she writhed helplessly. "I need you now."

He took her at her word, shifting over her, taking her lips in the same instant that he positioned himself between her parted thighs. He drove into her without hesitation, a groan of disbelief escaping him as he sank into her heated depths. She cried out and gripped his shoulders. Submerged in her consuming inner fire, Craig shuddered when he felt the possessive clutch of her body in the tiny muscles that tremored around his arousal.

With their bodies locked together, Craig stopped fighting the inevitable. He thrust deeply, repeatedly, pleasure rolling over him in waves and nearly swamping his conscious-ness as Chelsea met and answered his fast-paced thrusts with counterthrusts.

"Perfect," he muttered in disbelief when she suddenly stiffened, twisted against him, and then convulsed around him.

She cried out in ecstasy. Her climax lasted so long and milked his flesh so thoroughly that Craig lost control, his own release explosively violent and more sustained than ever before.

He collapsed atop her. She wept in silence. Although he felt the damp trail of her tears when he kissed her cheek, he didn't possess the will to chide her for being overly emotional.

They held each other, too dazed to speak, aftershocks tremoring through their bodies. Craig kept their bodies joined even after he rolled them onto their sides.

Chelsea dozed in his arms. He drifted off

eventually, forgetting the threat of his night-mares. When he awoke a short while later, it was not to panic, as was his nightly curse, but to the stunning sensations caused by Chelsea as she made love to him with her hands and mouth.

She tantalized him, she delighted him, and she repeatedly satisfied him as the night unfold-ed. When he thought he lacked the strength even to fill his lungs with much needed oxygen, let alone perform once more, his hunger for her returned tenfold.

Their mouths met by instinct, rather than by design, then parted, but only briefly.

They explored. They aroused. They pro-voked. They burned for each other, and then they eagerly quenched the flames that licked at them.

Neither held back. Secrets became revela-tions. Revelations became new avenues to mutu-al pleasure.

They pushed aside conventional bounda-ries, abandoned rules, discarded inhibitions, and embraced every erotic fantasy they'd ever had, experimenting in new and unique ways that produced laughter, breathless shock, and stunning pleasure. Their bodies blended again and again, and their never-ending passion for each other swept them into a series of turbulent matings that always ended with intense and very mutual satisfaction.

As he plundered the depths of Chelsea's body one last time, the dawn finally edged into the sky beyond the curtainless window in Craig's bedroom.

She trembled as her release swept through her, and she cried, "I love you!"

Stunned, Craig went spinning out of control, his body spasming with violence, his heart twisting painfully in his chest, and his emotions so devastated that he feared he might never recover from the loss he knew he was about to suffer.

Although deeply saddened by Craig's aloof attitude the next morning, Chelsea respected his apparent need for silence as they had a light breakfast, separately bathed and dressed, and then drove the three miles to her car. She longed to remain with him, even if it meant abandoning her life in San Francisco, but she knew now that he wouldn't ever permit her that luxury. She believed that he was too stubborn to forgive the sins he still credited to her. She also sensed his determination never to trust anyone he perceived as a threat to his survival, and she concluded that Craig had sentenced himself to the mountain cabin as some kind of misguided means of protecting himself.

She felt heartsick over his decision. She sighed softly as he guided the Jeep along the rutted road, the sound she made only a faint echo of her own deep inner turmoil and pain. She glanced at Craig, memorizing once more his rugged profile, the midnight fall of hair that cascaded past his shoulders, and the gold stud fastened to his earlobe. Her gaze skimmed hungrily over him. The desolate expression on his face, not simply the leashed power of his body, made her want to fling herself into his arms and plead with him for some kind of compromise that would permit them to begin anew.

Convinced that Craig would reject her request out of hand, Chelsea quelled the urge to speak, gripped the cracked edges of her seat cushion to keep from reaching out to him, and stared straight ahead. As they approached the makeshift bridge that spanned the ravine, Craig slowed the Jeep. Chelsea stiffened, her apprehension palpable as she warily eyed the structure.

As if sensing her anxiety, Craig halted the Jeep a few feet from the bridge. "There's no need to be afraid. I did several test crossings yesterday." He finally glanced at her, allowing her a glimpse of the myriad emotions that flashed across his face before he schooled his features to an expression of reassurance. "It's safe."

She nodded jerkily, feeling too tense and too near to sobbing to say anything as he put the Jeep into gear and eased onto the short bridge. Chelsea closed her eyes. She was unable to stop the images of her fall into the ravine. The new planks beneath the wheels of the Jeep moaned. As they traversed the lengths of bolted-down timber, Chelsea acknowledged the truth behind Craig's comment. Safely across, she loosened her hold on the seat cushion, flexing her fingers to ease the cramps caused by her fear. She hugged her shoulder bag to her chest, her thoughts quickly shifting back to Craig. Already mourning their impending, and very likely permanent, separation, she wondered if she would ever be able to move beyond the death of a relationship that had begun with so much hope and love eight years earlier.

After pulling into the clearing at the entrance to his land, Craig parked the Jeep next to the gate. He got out of the driver's seat without his usual physical grace, his body rigid as he walked around to the passenger side of the vehicle.

Chelsea pushed open the door, forgetting for a moment that while she wore the clothes she'd arrived in several days before, her shoes had disappeared when she'd tumbled into the ravine. A thick pair of Craig's wool socks covered her feet.

"I can walk," she protested, afraid that if he touched her she would unravel.

He replied with a meaningful glance at her feet, then reached for her, making short work of the walk to her car which was parked nearby. Craig tucked her into the low-slung sports car, stepped back, and closed the door, but he didn't walk away.

Setting aside her purse once she located her keys and slipped the ignition key into place, Chelsea lowered the window. "I don't regret coming here," she said, her manner subdued as she twisted in her seat and peered up at him.

"I suppose it was inevitable."

His concession stung, because it was offered in such a cold tone of voice. Chelsea fought the urge to tell him what a fool he was to cast her aside out of fear. Controlling her frustration, she decided instead to speak to him from her heart. "Don't hate me any longer, Craig. I couldn't bear it if I thought you did."

He nodded abruptly. "Have you got everything?"

"I traveled light this trip." She smiled faintly, recalling her tendency to overpack when they'd gone away for long weekends and vacations during their courtship and marriage. "Unlike in the past. You used to accuse me of trying to turn you into a pack mule."

"Don't, Chelsea. The past is gone, and our marriage is dead and buried. You can't get it or us back, no matter what you do or say."

She bit her lip, the reality of his words settling over her like a shroud. She turned the key in the ignition, and the expensive German auto purred to life.

"Do you have enough gas to get down the mountain? Do you need any money?"

"I'm fine on both counts," she whispered, stricken by the husbandly sound of his questions.

Craig stepped back, his entire demeanor as dismissive as the look on his hard-featured face. "Then you'd better be on your way."

"Craig?" she said as he backed away.

He paused, but he didn't meet her gaze. "What, Chelsea?" he asked, the sharp edge back in his voice again.

"Will you let me know how you're doing

from time to time? Perhaps we could meet for a cup of coffee and just talk every few months or so? We were friends before we were anything else," she reminded him.

She noticed immediately that he didn't bother to hide his distaste with her suggestions. Although he said nothing, Chelsea saw the coldness in his eyes and the way his mouth narrowed to a thin white line. She sighed, frustrated as much with him as with herself. "I should know better than to beg, shouldn't I?"

"Since you know what you're doing, why don't you stop it?" He shifted from foot to foot, clearly uncomfortable with her attempts to secure a promise from him that he couldn't give. "There's no point in staying in touch. I can't change what I've become, and you aren't capable of enduring a life with me on my terms."

"I'm not asking you to change."

"You're asking me to forgive and to trust, Chelsea. You might as well ask me to throw myself in front of a truck. It's not going to happen. Not ever."

Struggling for patience, she insisted, "I'm simply asking you to think about the benefits to yourself if you let go of the past and embrace the future."

"Then you let go of me first," he ground out, repeating her words to make his point. "You're suffocating me, and I can't handle much more of this."

Emotionally drained, she gathered up the remnants of her shredded dignity and met his hard gaze. "Even though we'll probably never see each other again, I really am glad I came to see you, and I'm glad we've had this time together. Take care of yourself, Craig. I'll miss you, and I'll think about you."

"Dammit!" he exploded as he approached her. "I can't do what you want! I can't be the person you need me to be." He slammed his fists on the roof of the sports car. "It's just not possible. I'm going to burn that journal, because I'd go insane if I had to rehash what happened." Leaning down, he gripped the rim of the car window. "Why won't you understand?"

"I do understand," Chelsea insisted stubbornly, her restraint disappearing once and for all. "I know exactly what you're risking if you reopen old wounds. I relive those months of hell on a regular basis, but I want you to heal, Craig, and healing means reading the journal so that you can undo some of the damage that's been done to you. Do it for your sake, not mine, and I'll do whatever I can to help you get your conviction overturned. I don't care if my father's reputation is ripped to pieces in open court, because he committed so many crimes against us that I've lost count of them all. You decide what you want to do, and I'll be at your side the entire time, but only if you want me there. You deserve a public forum when you have your name cleared, and this is your best option. I can't offer you anything else, other than my life, and I'd give that to you, too, if I thought it would make a difference."

He looked stunned. "Why, Chelsea? Why?"

She shook her head in amazement. "Because I love you. Because I will love you until the day I die."

Craig exhaled harshly, the sound weighted with emotional fatigue and tinged with uncertainty. Chelsea saw his disbelief, but she refused to let up on him now. "If you're going to have a future, you must come to terms with the past. It's that simple, but it's also that complicated."

He glared down at her. "Where did that little bit of wisdom come from? The back of a cereal box?"

She ignored his hostility. "Life! I lived through my own version of what happened to you, but you've very conveniently forgotten that fact, haven't you? Someday, if there ever is a someday for us, I'll tell you what happened to *me* six years ago. You need to hear my truths, my realities, but I'll save them until you're ready. Fair warning, Craig, because once you hear what I have to say, you won't be able to dismiss me any longer as one of the architects of your downfall."

"Get on with your life, Chelsea, and don't come back," he advised harshly, all the armor he used to protect his emotions locked into place again. "There's nothing here for you, and there never will be."

"Damn you, Craig Wilder, I'm sick to death of your paranoia where I'm concerned. I deserve your trust. I've always deserved it, but you're still so blasted self-involved that you wouldn't notice me if I fainted at your feet. You'd probably assume I was a curb and step over me. Enjoy your bitterness and solitude, because I've had enough of your hostility to last me the rest of my life."

Chelsea angrily shifted the car into gear and pulled out onto the sun-dappled road. She didn't bother to try to catch a last glimpse of Craig in the rearview mirror as she drove away, but only because her eyes had flooded with tears of frustration and sadness. She made it around the first bend in the road before she slowed the car, guided it onto the shoulder, and turned off the engine.

Covering her face with her hands, she wept for herself, for the baby she'd miscarried, and for Craig, whom she realized was lost to her forever. It was a long time before she felt strong enough to begin the return trip to San Francisco.

Rigid with tension, Craig watched Chelsea disappear from sight. He told himself that he was better off without her as he secured the gate to his property and stomped back to his Jeep, but he hesitated once he reached the vehicle, aware that he was lying to himself—just as he'd lied to her, his conscience reminded him. His broad shoulders slumped. Craig pressed the heels of his hands over his eyes, trying but failing to rationalize his cruelty to Chelsea.

I love you. I will love you until the day I die.

Why in hell had she said that to him? To strip him of his pride? To torture him? To remind him that without her his life had no real meaning? To force him to face the past and get it into proper perspective as the shrinks he'd gone to when he'd first left prison had urged him to do?

Craig swore viciously, added yet another

dent to the Jeep when he kicked the fender with his boot-covered foot, and then drove back to his cabin like a madman pursued by demons from hell.

In the days and weeks that followed, Craig vibrated with an inner fury that threatened his sanity. With his nerves coiled into knots, he didn't have a single moment of peace, whether awake or asleep. He couldn't summon his appetite, although he forced himself to eat at least once a day. He shouted his rage whenever it welled up inside him, recognizing but not caring after a while that he sounded like a mortally wounded animal.

He didn't completely understand why he failed to follow through on his threat to destroy Martin Lockridge's journal. Although he tossed it into the fireplace at one point, he retrieved it, burning his fingers as he rescued the scorched leather from flames licking at it. Some instinct prompted him to shove the journal into a kitchen drawer he rarely used and ignore it.

I love you.

Her words played through his mind like a never-ending chorus, haunting him day in and day out. The safety and serenity he'd once found in the mountain cabin disappeared like a puff of smoke subjected to a hard wind. He saw Chelsea everywhere he looked, and he cursed her for having invaded his privacy in the first place.

He heard the sound of her soft laughter at odd moments. He found himself frozen in place, regardless of the task he pursued, when he remembered her moans of shocked pleasure each time she'd climaxed in his arms. He cursed the memories and himself, but he still recalled every deliciously sensual curve and hollow of her body and the ecstasy he'd experienced when he achieved his release while embedded in her body or as a result of her clever, loving mouth.

Most nights, he dozed on the floor in front of the fireplace before dragging himself off to bed, where he tossed and turned, unable to sleep because his body constantly hungered for her. He reached for her in the darkness during those rare moments when he did manage to fall asleep, but he awakened empty-handed and frustrated. He smelled her unique fragrance on his pillow, even after he stripped the sheets from his bed and laundered them. His nightmares intensified to the point that he refused even to consider resting unless he was staggering from exhaustion.

When he wasn't chopping firewood, patching the roof of the cabin, working on the plot for his garden, or dreaming up other chores for himself, Craig prowled the woods, his thoughts chaotic, his emotions growing increasingly more fragmented.

Three weeks after Chelsea's departure, Craig pulled the journal from the kitchen drawer and read the contents. He relived every grim moment of his indictment, the trial that followed, the guilty verdict, and his prison term. Although he had difficulty reconciling her past behavior with the compassion and patience she'd displayed during their time together at his cabin, Craig chalked up the changes in Chelsea to a level of maturity and clear-sightedness she'd apparently gained since her father's death.

He learned exactly how he'd been framed for jury tampering, and he learned why. He read the dead man's plea for forgiveness, but he remained unmoved. He doubted his ability to forgive or to stop hating his former father-in-law, because he finally saw the older man for what he'd been—an ambitious, self-serving creature, who willingly sacrificed anyone, including his only daughter, in his pursuit of success and acclaim as a federal prosecutor.

Despite the shock and anger that consumed

him for several days, Craig recognized the legal options open to him if he presented Lockridge's confession to the appropriate authorities. He also realized the enormity of the sacrifice that Chelsea had made in giving him the journal, because she'd been victimized too.

He desperately wanted her back in his life. He found the strength and courage within himself to forgive her for betraying him when he came to terms with the degree to which they'd both been used and manipulated by her father. Craig acknowledged, as well, the wisdom of her advice that he confront the past once and for all. He finally understood and accepted the idea that unless he achieved some sense of closure, he would never experience any peace in the future.

Craig contacted his parole officer and a San Francisco attorney he respected, initiating the steps necessary to clear his name and at least partially restore his reputation.

He loved and needed Chelsea too much not to try to win her back. He also wanted to understand what she'd meant about her *truths* and her *realities*.

TEN

The doorchimes peeled. Chelsea paused on the staircase, surprised that anyone would be calling on her at such an early hour. She crossed the foyer, tugged aside the semisheer drape that covered the beveled glass insert in the mahogany front door, and peered at the man who stood with his back to her on the front porch.

He turned, as though sensing her presence, and met her gaze. Chelsea blinked, unable to believe her eyes. Clad in a crisp white, button-down shirt open at the throat, navy trousers and matching corduroy sport jacket, and a pair of western-style leather boots, Craig looked as though he'd just stepped from the pages of a men's fashion magazine.

She noted, too, that his hair was still long,

although it had been trimmed. Minus his bandanna, the black mane flowed freely to his shoulders. His rugged facial features, not just his powerful body, served to emphasize his overwhelming masculinity, and she suddenly realized that he appeared calmer than he'd been during their time together in the mountains.

Drawing in a steadying breath, Chelsea let the drape fall back into place, unlocked the door, and pulled it open. She clutched the doorknob, too disturbed to do or say anything, even though she'd prayed for two months that he'd come to her.

"Did I wake you?" Craig asked.

"No!" she exclaimed nervously. "I've been up for an hour or so."

"I realize it's early, but I need to talk to you. You were right when you accused me of being self-involved. I've been so wrapped up in my own concerns, I never took the time to ask how you were affected by the trial and our divorce, but I'm asking now, Chelsea, and I'm ready to listen to what you have to say."

Although stunned, she stepped aside. "Come in."

Her gaze stayed riveted on Craig as he walked into the foyer of the house she'd inherited from her father. Chelsea closed the door and leaned back against it, absently placing her hand over her middle, and swallowed against the sudden queasiness stirring her stomach.

Craig turned to look at her, then frowned. "You're awfully pale. Are you all right?"

She nodded and straightened, determined not to be sick in front of him. "I'm fine. The coffee maker's ready to be turned on. Would you like a cup?"

"Sounds good."

Chelsea crossed the foyer, the black silk caftan she wore molding to her shapely body as she walked ahead of Craig. She kept her distance, although she paused and glanced back at him when she heard his footsteps slow. She saw then that his attention had been snagged by the living room.

"I like the changes you've made."

"The dark paneling and heavy velvet drapes were depressing, so I remodeled the interior of the house after Dad passed away, auctioned off all of his furnishings, and took our things out of storage."

"You always favored crisp white walls, vaulted ceilings, and plantation-style shutters if the windows had to be covered."

"Shades of the claustrophobia I had as a child, I suspect."

While Chelsea grappled with his unannounced visit and his polite remarks, Craig behaved like a browser at an art exhibit as he walked down the wide hallway that led to the kitchen. Chelsea noticed his fascination with the gallery-style display she'd created with some of the artwork they'd collected during their marriage. She stood in the doorway of the kitchen when he lingered in front of a trio of impressionist nudes.

"I'm glad you saved the prints."

"We bought them on our honeymoon," she reminded him, secretly pleased that he remembered the collection. He glanced at her, then away. She wondered why he suddenly looked so strained.

"A happier time," he finally remarked as he followed her into the remodeled kitchen with its stark white walls and appliances, its teal and mauve counter and floor tiles. "Aren't these the same colors we had in our kitchen at the condo?"

"I'm surprised you remember."

"I remember a lot of things now, Chelsea, especially your ability to be compassionate and kind."

She frowned, unprepared for his compliment, but she managed to remember the manners ingrained in her by the people hired to raise her after her mother's death. "Thank you."

"I've made some decisions I'd like to share with you."

"All right," she whispered.

She removed a dish towel from the counter-top near the sink, unconsciously gripping it with both hands as she crossed the room to the coffee maker. After turning it on, she faced Craig, who stood on the opposite side of the spacious room.

"I don't have to work today, so we have plenty of time."

"You're going to shred the dish towel if you keep twisting it that way."

Chelsea stared at Craig. The towel fell from her hands. He crossed the room, collected the dropped towel from the floor, and slid it onto the counter behind her. He stood so close that she stopped breathing for a moment, her hands once again making their way to the front of her body.

His eyes narrowed as he studied her. Chelsea thought he looked unsettled, perhaps even dismayed. Ruddy color stained his high cheekbones.

"You're trembling. If I'm making you uncomfortable, I can leave."

She shook her head in denial. "No, that's all right. I'm just tired. I didn't sleep very well last night."

"You're nervous, Chelsea. I know the difference between fatigue and nerves where you're concerned."

"I'm shocked to see you, that's all."

"I should have called first."

She reached out, grazed the sleeve of his jacket with her fingertips, and then withdrew her hand. "No, I'm glad you decided to drop in. You look very handsome."

"I finally bought some decent clothes," he said with an embarrassed laugh. "I wanted you to see for yourself that I'm doing better, especially since I finally took your advice."

"You read the journal?"

"It took me a few weeks, but I read it. I've hired an attorney to handle my case. We're petitioning the court for a hearing in order to have the new evidence reviewed. It'll take time, but Tom seems confident that my conviction will be overturned and that I'll eventually be reinstated by the bar association."

"Oh, Craig, I'm so glad. You seemed so determined to ignore the journal. What changed your mind?"

"You."

"That's not possible. You rejected my help," she reminded him. "You said I was smothering you, you didn't answer my letters, and you hung up on me the two times I called you. I didn't help you. If anything, I annoyed and angered you."

"I wasn't ready to talk to you when you called. I am now. I also wanted to speak to you face-to-face. I couldn't put my feelings in a letter."

"You're sleeping better now, aren't you?"

He nodded. "Once I read the journal, I stopped having the nightmares. The books you sent helped too. I'm learning how to redirect my anger by channeling it into things I can control."

Staggered by his admission that she'd some-how managed to provide the incentive he needed to take control of his life, she felt almost faint. "Why don't we go into the breakfast room and sit down while we wait for the coffee to brew?"

"Lead the way."

They sat opposite each other on the broad window seat that offered a panoramic view of San Francisco Bay. "Do you still grind your own beans?"

She half smiled at his attempt at small talk, even though she recalled how he'd teased her in the past about freshly ground beans for their coffee. "It's a small luxury, but one I enjoy."

Glancing out the window, Craig unknowingly offered his profile for her inspection. Chelsea couldn't take her eyes off him, nor could she decide what to do with her hands, because she wanted to reach out and touch the warmth and resilience of his muscular body. She tangled her fingers together in her lap instead and simply watched him.

"I'd forgotten how beautiful the view is of the bay from here. It was still dark when I crossed the bridge this morning."

"I sit in here at night and watch the boat traffic. I have the same view from my bedroom. It's a nice way to begin or end a day."

"I wouldn't have recognized the interior of the house." He exhaled, the sound oddly vulnerable as he looked at her. "What happened to our place?"

The memory saddened her, but she didn't try to protect Craig with a lie. "I had to sell it in order to pay your lawyer. Dad refused to help me make the mortgage payments or cosign a loan when I ran out of money, but I inherited this house and several pieces of rental property when he died. I guess he felt he'd provided for me well enough."

If Craig noticed her resentment, or if he felt any himself, he didn't comment. "You're in a better neighborhood now."

"True, but the house is too big. I've been thinking about renting some of the bedrooms to students at the Art Institute."

"I'm surprised that you'd consider giving up your privacy, especially if you're entertaining the way we used to."

She shook her head. "I can't remember the last time I gave a party. I withdrew from all the social, civic, and political causes long ago. Looking back, I realize how much I hated planning parties for people I hardly knew or didn't even like. It was just something I was expected to do for Dad, and then for you. Working part-time for the child custody division and doing volunteer work at the hospital provided me with the chance to get off that merry-go-round, so I took it."

"No social life at all?" he asked, his expression and tone of voice tentative.

She thought about her conversation with her doctor the previous day, and his news that she was nine weeks pregnant. She also recalled how devastated she'd been for the last few months. Since last seeing Craig, she'd holed up in the house, leaving only when she needed to buy food or meet her commitments at the child custody division or at the hospital.

Studying Craig now with a tender gaze, Chelsea realized yet again how very much she loved this man, and how difficult it was to accept that her life, and the life of the child they'd created, wouldn't include him. Despite how unlikely and unrealistic her dreams, she still secretly harbored the hope that they would find their way back to each other.

"Chelsea?"

She snapped back to the present. "No, Craig, no social life to speak of."

He clamped his jaws together and looked away, as if he needed to get himself under control before he spoke again. She waited, puzzled by his behavior, but willing to be patient with him.

"I've been working for the last three weeks. It feels good to have my hands on my old law books. Thank you for shipping them to me."

"I hoped they'd remind you that you were a good lawyer once upon a time, and that you will be again. Are you going to try for reinstatement at the federal prosecutor's office when your conviction is overturned?"

"When?"

"*When*," Chelsea confirmed, her chin tilting to a stubborn angle. "It's just a matter of time."

Craig smiled, the first genuine smile she'd seen on his face in years. "I may need you to share some of your confidence."

"I have plenty to spare."

"I've been hired as a legal advocate for inmates who've been incarcerated following questionable due process. I'll probably stick with it, regardless of the outcome in court."

"They're fortunate to have you. I hope you enjoy the work, and I know you'll do a first-rate job for your clients."

Craig moved closer, reached out, and took her hands. He gently separated her fingers before closing his hands over them. "Where does your confidence in me come from? I've given you a thousand and one reasons to hate me, and yet you still manage to be generous with your praise and encouragement. I don't understand how you do it, Chelsea."

Frightened that she might fling herself into his arms and confess her love, she reluctantly freed herself, shrugging with a carelessness she didn't really feel as she got up from the window seat. She felt Craig's gaze as she wandered across the room, turned, and then looked at him. She placed her hand on her stomach in a protective gesture, which drew a frown from Craig.

"Is your stomach bothering you again?"

Her hands slid down to her sides. "No. Are you staying in the city now?"

His frown deepened, but he merely answered her question. "I have an apartment in Berkeley, but I go up to the cabin on the weekends. I still need the quiet and the space. I suspect I always will."

"Will you need my help when your attorney goes into court?"

"Yes."

"Just have him contact me. There's a trust fund that's been set up for your legal expenses. You have to promise me that you'll use it, Craig."

"That's not necessary."

"Promise me, please."

"If it means that much to you, I'll use the trust fund."

She lifted her hands and pressed her fingertips to her forehead as she began to pace again. "It means everything to me, because it will allow you to vindicate yourself."

"I want you to understand what's involved before you agree to testify," Craig said, caution in his voice. "You'll be subjected to a lot of questions about the personal side of what happened to us, since it's your father who set me up. I can swing this thing on my own if you'd prefer to stay out of it. I don't want you hurt, Chelsea. You've been through enough."

Suddenly unable to take another step, she lowered herself into the nearest chair. She wanted him to put his arms around her and tell her that he still loved her. She wanted to tell him that they'd made another baby during those tumultuous days they'd shared at the cabin.

Instead, she put aside her needs, not just her disappointment that he couldn't see she'd do anything to help him. "I'm prepared to handle whatever is revealed in court, but are you? I have some revelations of my own that may shock you."

How will you feel when you discover that I was carrying our child? she wondered. *Will you even want the baby I'm carrying now?*

"I want the truth known, but not at your expense. It'll be tough, Chelsea, because the hearing will be open to the public."

"The media," she whispered, recalling how they'd hounded her six years before, camping out in front of the condominium, following her to the grocery store, trailing after her, microphones shoved into her face as she walked into the courtroom. Chelsea squared her shoulders, vowing not to be intimidated by strangers. "I'll deal with whatever I have to deal with. We'll make this work out for you, I promise."

"My attorney wants to do a preliminary interview with you."

"When and where?"

"Here, if you'd like, and as soon as possible. I wanted your permission, though, before I authorize him to call you." He hesitated. "You'll need a lawyer when you're deposed and when you testify."

"I won't need anyone if you're at my side," she insisted.

He gave her a look of surprise. "I'll be there, if that's what you want."

"I trust you, Craig." She got to her feet and began to roam around the room. She breathed slowly in and out as she tried to calm her stomach and her nerves.

"I need to understand why you weren't there for me at the end, Chelsea. It's the part of our situation that I've never been able to come to terms with. Didn't you love me enough to stand by me? Didn't you believe that I was innocent?"

Shocked by his questions, she stumbled to a stop, turned a sickly shade of green, and grabbed at the wall for support as she stared at him.

He shot to his feet, his long-legged stride eating up the space that separated them. Slipping his arms around her, he stabilized her and walked her in the direction of the nearest chair. "Chelsea?"

"How can you ask me such questions? I loved you more than my life. And I believed in you the way I believe in God's grace and mercy."

"I had to ask, and I realize now that I don't have a clue about what you went through. I'm here because I think you have things to tell me, things I need to know, the things you called truths and realities. I want to hear them now."

She groaned. "No."

"Look, you're the one who stopped coming to court when my defense began to collapse like a house of cards. All I remember is that I needed you, and you weren't there. Your father said you thought I was guilty. He told me you wanted a divorce even before the verdict came back."

"That's insane. I was ill. I nearly died. When I was conscious, I became hysterical because I couldn't get to you. They restrained me." The memory was still powerful enough to make her physically ill. "They strapped me to a bed in order to stop me from trying to leave the hospital."

He stared at her. "What in hell are you talking about?"

"I was in the hospital. St. Mary's. Your bail had been revoked for several weeks by then, and you were spending your days and nights as a guest of the federal authorities," she said softly. "The doctors were trying to keep me quiet, because I kept calling for you. I tried to get to you, Craig. I tried, and I tried . . . but I kept failing. They tranquilized me. I'd lose hours, sometimes days at a stretch."

Tears filled her eyes, but she dashed them away. Sliding free of his loose embrace, she started moving around the room again. "My father . . . my father told me you didn't want me, that you didn't care about me. I learned later that he'd persuaded the doctors not to notify you, and he had the influence to make his orders stick."

Craig grabbed her shoulder and swung her around. "Stop pacing and look at me. You're about to pass out. You're also not making much sense, Chelsea."

She waved him off as she fled his hands. "I *am* making sense. You weren't there. You don't know how awful it was. I fell. That's how I lost the baby," she said, the words and emotions pouring out of her at a reckless pace. "You didn't try to find me. You believed my father when he told you I didn't love you. Why did you believe him? Why?" She moaned. "You were my whole life."

Craig stopped her before she ran out of the room, grabbing her from behind, holding her against his chest despite her brief struggle to free herself. He laced his arms around her waist and lowered his head. "What baby?" he demanded, his voice so cold, it sounded lethal.

"Our baby," Chelsea whispered brokenly. "My father promised me that he'd bring you to me, but then he told me you'd refused to come to the hospital even though the judge had authorized a visit. He told me you didn't want anything to do with me after I miscarried." She shivered, and a sob shuddered through her. "Oh God, I needed you so much, but you weren't there." She twisted in his arms and raised tear-flooded eyes to his face. "You needed me too. I'm sure you did, but I couldn't get to you no matter how hard I tried."

"Our baby?" he repeated, shock leeching much of the natural color from his face. "You were pregnant? You fell? When? How? Tell me what happened, Chelsea."

She sagged in his arms, her head dropping against his shoulder. "A neighbor found me. I thought I heard someone trying to break into the condo in the middle of the night. I went to investigate, and I tripped. I fell down a flight of stairs."

"Why in God's name didn't you tell me you were pregnant?"

She gripped his arms. "Please try to understand. I couldn't. I would have just added to the pressure you were under. I didn't find out about my pregnancy until after you were arrested. The timing was awful. You were so worried then, and you were trying to help your lawyer. I always believed that you'd be set free, so I decided to save my wonderful news for the day the jury came in with a not-guilty verdict. By the time everything was over, by the time the baby was gone and I was released from the hospital, you'd been sentenced and taken to prison. I wanted to tell you. I tried and tried for months, but you wouldn't see me. The warden finally asked me not to come back. He said I was making a nuisance of myself."

"That's why you kept visiting the prison," he said breathlessly. "I couldn't figure it out. I thought you were trying to punish me by reminding me of what I'd lost."

"Once you filed for divorce," she continued, "I realized that telling you about the baby wouldn't change anything. You didn't want me, and I couldn't have handled any more rejection. I was on the verge of a breakdown."

"A breakdown?" His fingers dug into her arms.

Chelsea swayed unsteadily. Craig swung her up against his broad chest. Placing her on the couch in the living room, he sat beside her and circled her shoulders with his arm. Neither spoke for several minutes.

"Your father really did a hell of a job on us, didn't he?"

She felt the fury that vibrated through him. Tears streamed from her eyes and trailed down her cheeks. Despite her own emotional upset, Chelsea felt Craig pulling into himself, distancing himself from her as they sat together. She grabbed his hand, fearful because she remembered his penchant for walking away from difficult conversations during their stay at the cabin. "I'm sorry. If I could change what happened, I would."

"I'll be back." He stood abruptly and headed for the front door.

"No!" she cried. In spite of how badly she was shaking, Chelsea ran after him, dashing ahead of him before he could intercept her and flattening herself against the door so that he couldn't open it. "Don't you dare run away from me. You can't deal with this alone, Craig, and I refuse to be abandoned again."

Hands fisted at his sides, he ordered, "Get the hell out of my way, Chelsea. I need some fresh air. I said I'd be back."

She shook her head. "I don't believe you." Tugging open the door, she parked her body in the center of the doorway like a crossing guard. "Take a deep breath. Take twenty if you need to, but don't run from me. We can get through this together. I understand the shock and grief you feel. I survived it, and I know you can too."

Craig hesitated, his inner struggle painfully obvious to her as he grappled with his emotions and tried to keep them in check. She watched him triumph over the rage and panic that made his body as rigid as a slab of stone. She felt proud that he'd accomplished the feat, but she sensed that other emotions, emotions that he might consider unmanly, simmered just below his rugged surface.

Craig reached for her, surprising her when he curved his hands over her shoulders. She welcomed his touch, the physical connection he initiated allaying some of her fears that he might feel inclined to cut and run without warning. Stepping forward, she slid her arms around his waist, pressed her cheek to his chest, and listened to the frantic beating of his heart.

When he finally wrapped his arms around her and held on to her as though she'd become his lifeline, she breathed yet another shaky sigh of relief. "I was in a deep depression after the divorce. I couldn't sleep, I couldn't eat, and I couldn't think straight for months. Dad ignored me. By then, all of our so-called friends had disappeared. I passed out in the elevator at the condominium one day, and when I woke up I was in the hospital again. They kept me there for almost two months. Dad told them I'd always been unstable and that I needed psychiatric care, but my doctor recognized my grief for what it was and eventually released me for outpatient care. I received counseling for almost two years. The process was painful, but I had a lot of things to resolve. Even though it seemed to take forever, I eventually came to terms with what had happened to me, to our marriage, and to the baby."

She looked up at Craig, saw the emotions he couldn't control welling in his beautiful dark eyes. Her heart broke for him as he fought with his pain, but she kept trying to penetrate the armor that he used to protect his emotions.

"Along the way I learned that it's all right to mourn the past. The key to surviving it is not to let yourself make too many return trips, because you risk getting lost there forever. You have to do the same thing, Craig. You have to let go of everything you couldn't control or prevent from happening in the past, so that you can have the future. I'll help you, I promise. I'll stand by you, I'll listen whenever you need to talk. I'll hold you in my arms when you've run out of words and just need to be comforted because you feel like you're being torn apart inside. I'll do for you what no one was willing or able to do for me, because I know how important it is to be reassured and loved. Even though I've become an unwilling expert on grief, I've figured out how to live without fear and not be haunted by a past I haven't got the power to change."

Although she didn't realize it at first, her words sent him over the edge, and he finally gave in to his emotions. He also accepted the comfort Chelsea offered. He wept as they stood in the doorway, his head bowed, his strong body shaken by the sobs that ripped through his large frame. Chelsea held him, convinced that he needed to express his feelings despite how awkward he might feel later.

She cried with him, but she didn't cry for the past. She shed her tears for the uncertainty ahead of them, because she wanted and needed to be a part of his life, even though she refused to delude herself into thinking that a future together was truly possible. She still doubted that Craig would ever risk giving her his complete trust, and without trust she knew there couldn't be mutual, enduring love.

Chelsea didn't know how long they stood there, and she really didn't care. She focused completely on Craig, who slowly regained his composure.

"How did you do it?" he finally asked. "Where does your strength come from, Chelsea?"

"I'm not that strong. I'm just stubborn as all hell."

"You are that," he agreed. He covered his face with his hands, then shoved his fingers through his hair. Refocusing on her upraised face, he searched her features for several moments, then touched the side of her cheek with trembling fingers. "After what I've put you through, why don't you hate the sight of me?"

"You didn't put me through anything. My father had that dubious honor. Besides, what would hatred accomplish?" she asked with characteristic tenderness, despite how drained she felt. "Would it restore our love and resurrect our marriage? Would it have made my father a better person? Would it have saved our baby's life?" Chelsea shook her head. "It can't do any of those things. Hatred simply destroys, and there's been enough damage done to us already."

"You should hate me," Craig insisted roughly, full of self-loathing. "Why don't you?"

She sighed, recognizing with no small amount of amazement that he still didn't understand the strength and depth of her love for him. "You should know the answer to that by now."

"Have I lost you, Chelsea? Have I been so stupid and so cruel that I've managed to lose you?"

"I told you that I loved you, and I meant what I said. I've never stopped loving you, so you couldn't get rid of me if you wanted to, but don't get the wrong idea about me. I'm no martyr, nor am I a saint, and I'm not kidding myself. If we're going to have a chance at friendship, or anything else that might evolve, we have to be honest with each other. No more hiding. No more games. We've both had enough of that kind of behavior."

"I want you," he said, his voice raw with emotion.

"Then have me," she said with heartfelt sincerity. "There's nothing I want more right now."

He pulled her out of the doorway, kicked the door shut and locked it, and then led her up the stairs. Understanding his need for reassurance and his desire to express his emotions on a physical level, Chelsea guided him to her bedroom.

They watched each other as they shed their clothes, then simultaneously reached out, coming together with sighs of relief and moans of anticipation as their warm and already aroused bodies melted together.

Holding her in his arms, Craig vowed, "I love you more than anyone or anything in this world. I will always love you, Chelsea Lockridge Wilder. Promise me that someday you'll be my wife again. Promise me that you'll make babies with me when the time is right. Promise me that you'll share your dreams with me, and then laugh with me as we grow old together."

She flung her arms around his neck. "Yes! Yes! Yes! A thousand times yes!"

They sank down onto the bed together, mouths meeting, hands stroking, and bodies blending to form one. He loved her with all the passion that had built up inside of him during their two months apart. She loved him back with tenderness and an innate sensuality that was as instinctive to her as breathing.

Much later, once they'd collapsed across the bed, Chelsea breathlessly asked, "Is this the right time?"

Still sprawled over her, Craig lifted his face from the scented curve of her neck. "Is it the right time for what?"

"A baby?"

Craig jerked in surprise, then rolled free of her. He tugged her against his side and hesitantly, but very possessively curved his hand over the gentle rise of her stomach. "Are you?"

Chelsea nodded, her pale face wreathed by a wide smile. "Nine weeks."

He gathered her into his arms, vowing, "Then we'll make it the right time, little one. We'll make it our time."

Craig followed her when she dashed into the bathroom a short while later. Once she felt better, he bathed her forehead with a cool, damp cloth, tucked her into bed, and went down to the kitchen to make weak tea and dry toast. As he prepared to care for his woman, the woman who would bear this child and the others they would have in the years ahead, Craig Wilder realized that he'd been given a second chance at happiness with Chelsea. He didn't intend to waste it.

THE EDITOR'S
CORNER

The bounty of six LOVESWEPTs coming your way next month is sure to put you in the right mood for the holiday season. Emotional and exciting, sensuous and scintillating, these tales of love and romance guarantee hours of unbeatable reading pleasure. So indulge yourself—there's no better way to start the celebration!

Leading our lineup is Charlotte Hughes with **KISSED BY A ROGUE**, LOVESWEPT #654—and a rogue is exactly what Cord Buford is. With a smile that promises wicked pleasures, he's used to getting what he wants, so when the beautiful new physician in town insists she won't go out with him, he takes it as a very personal challenge. He'll do anything to feel Billie Foster's soft hands on him, even dare her to give him a physical. Billie's struggle to resist Cord's dangerous temptations is useless, but when their investigation into a mystery at his family's textile mill erupts into steamy kisses under moonlit skies, she has to wonder if she's the one woman who can tame his wild heart. Charlotte's talent shines brightly in this delicious romance.

New author Debra Dixon makes an outstanding debut in LOVESWEPT with **TALL, DARK, AND LONESOME**, #655. Trail boss Zach Weston is definitely all of those things, as Niki Devlin soon discovers when she joins his vacation cattle drive. The columnist starts out interested only in getting a story, but from the moment Zach pulls her out of the mud and into his arms, she wants to scorch his iron control and play with the fire in his gray eyes. However, she believes the scandal that haunts her past can destroy his dreams of happily-ever-after—until Zach dares her to stop running and be lassoed by his love. Talented Debra combines emotional intensity and humor to make **TALL, DARK, AND LONESOME** a winner. You're sure to look forward to more from this New Face of 1993!

Do you remember Jenny Love-Townsend, the heroine's daughter in Peggy Webb's **TOUCHED BY ANGELS**? She returns in **A PRINCE FOR JENNY**, LOVESWEPT #656, but now she's all grown up, a fragile artist who finally meets the man of her dreams. Daniel Sullivan is everything she's ever wished for and the one thing she's sure she can't have. Daniel agrees that the spellbinding emotion between them can't last. He doesn't consider himself to be as noble, strong, and powerful as Jenny sketched him, and though he wants to taste her magic, his desire for this special woman can put her in danger. Peggy will have you crying and cheering as these two people find the courage to believe in the power of love.

What an apt title **FEVER** is for Joan J. Domning's new LOVESWEPT #657, for the temperature does nothing but rise when Alec Golightly and Bunny Fletcher meet. He's a corporate executive who wears a Hawaiian shirt and a pirate's grin—not at all what she expects when she goes to Portland to help bail out his company. Her plan is to get the job done, then quickly return to the fast track, but she suddenly finds herself wildly tempted to run into his arms and stay there. A family is one thing she's never had time for in her race to be the best, but with Alec tantalizing her with his long, slow kisses, she's ready to seize the happiness that has always eluded her. Joan delivers a sexy romance that burns white-hot with desire.

Please welcome Jackie Reeser and her very first novel, **THE LADY CASTS HER LURES**, LOVESWEPT #658. Jackie's a veteran journalist, and she has given her heroine, Pat Langston, the same occupation—and a vexing assignment: to accompany champion Brian Culler on the final round of a fishing contest. He's always found reporters annoying, but one look at Pat and he quickly welcomes the delectable distraction, baiting her with charm that could reel any woman in. The spirited single mom isn't interested in a lady's man who'd never settle down, though. But Brian knows all about being patient and pursues her with seductive humor, willing to wait for the prize of her passion. This delightful romance, told with plenty of verve and sensuality, will show you why we're so excited to be publishing Jackie in LOVESWEPT.

Diane Pershing rounds out the lineup in a very big way with **HEARTQUAKE**, LOVESWEPT #659. A golden-haired geologist, David Franklin prowls the earth in search of the secrets that make it tremble, but he's never felt a tremor as strong as the one that shakes his very soul when he meets Bella Stein. A distant relative, she's surprised by his arrival on her doorstep—and shocked by the restless longing he awakens in her. His wildfire caresses make the beautiful widow respond to him with shameless abandon. Then she discovers the pain he's hidden from everyone, and only her tenderness can heal him and show him that he's worthy of her gift of enduring love. . . . Diane's evocative writing makes this romance stand out.

Happy reading,

With warmest wishes,

Nita Taublib

Nita Taublib

Associate Publisher

P.S. Don't miss the spectacular women's novels Bantam has coming in December: **ADAM'S FALL** by Sandra Brown, a classic romance soon to be available in hardcover; **NOTORIOUS** by Patricia Potter, in which the rivalry and passion between two saloon owners becomes the rage of San Francisco; **PRINCESS OF THIEVES** by Katherine O'Neal, featuring a delightfully wicked con woman and a rugged, ruthless bounty hunter; and **CAPTURE THE NIGHT** by Geralyn Dawson, the latest Once Upon a Time romance with "Beauty and the Beast" at its heart. We'll be giving you a sneak peak at these terrific books in next month's LOVESWEPTs. And immediately following this page, look for a preview of the exciting women's fiction from Bantam *available now!*

Don't miss these exciting books by your favorite Bantam authors

On sale in October:
OUTLAW
by Susan Johnson

MOONLIGHT, MADNESS, & MAGIC
by Suzanne Forster, Charlotte Hughes, and Olivia Rupprecht

SATIN AND STEELE
by Fayrene Preston

And in hardcover from Doubleday
SOMETHING BORROWED, SOMETHING BLUE
by Jillian Karr

"Susan Johnson brings sensuality to
new heights and beyond."
—*Romantic Times*

Susan Johnson

Nationally bestselling author of
SINFUL and **SILVER FLAME**

Outlaw

*Susan Johnson's most passionate and richly textured
romance yet, OUTLAW is the sizzling story of a fierce
Scottish border lord who abducts his sworn enemy, a
beautiful English woman—only to find himself a captive
of her love.*

"Come sit by me then." Elizabeth gently patted
the rough bark beside her as if coaxing a small child
to an unpleasant task.

He should leave, Johnnie thought. He shouldn't
have ridden after her, he shouldn't be panting like
a dog in heat for any woman . . . particularly for
this woman, the daughter of Harold Godfrey, his
lifelong enemy.

"Are you afraid of me?" She'd stopped running
now from her desire. It was an enormous leap of
faith, a rash and venturesome sensation for a woman who'd always viewed the world with caution.

"I'm not afraid of anything," Johnnie answered,
unhesitating confidence in his deep voice.

"I didn't think so," she replied. Dressed like a reiver in leather breeches, high boots, a shirt open at the throat, his hunting plaid the muted color of autumn foliage, he looked not only unafraid but menacing. The danger and attraction of scandalous sin, she thought—all dark arrogant masculinity. "My guardsmen will wait indefinitely," she said very, very quietly, thinking with an arrogance of her own, There. That should move him.

And when he took that first step, she smiled a tantalizing female smile, artless and instinctive.

"You please me," she said, gazing up at him as he slowly drew near.

"*You* drive me mad," Johnnie said, sitting down on the fallen tree, resting his arms on his knees and contemplating the dusty toes of his boots.

"And you don't like the feeling."

"I dislike it intensely," he retorted, chafing resentment plain in his voice.

He wouldn't look at her. "Would you rather I leave?"

His head swiveled toward her then, a cynical gleam in his blue eyes. "Of course not."

"Hmmm," Elizabeth murmured, pursing her lips, clasping her hands together and studying her yellow kidskin slippers. "This *is* awkward," she said after a moment, amusement in her voice. Sitting up straighter, she half turned to gaze at him. "I've never seduced a man before." A smile of unalloyed innocence curved her mouth. "Could you help me? If you don't mind, my lord," she demurely added.

A grin slowly creased his tanned cheek. "You play the ingenue well, Lady Graham," he said, sitting upright to better meet her frankly sensual gaze. His pale blue eyes had warmed, restoring a goodly measure of his charm. "I'd be a damned fool to mind," he said, his grin in sharp contrast to the curious affection in his eyes.

Exhaling theatrically, Elizabeth said, "Thank you, my lord," in a blatant parody of gratitude. "Without your assistance I despaired of properly arousing you."

He laughed, a warm-hearted sound of natural pleasure. "On that count you needn't have worried. I've been in rut since I left Edinburgh to see you."

"Could I be of some help?" she murmured, her voice husky, enticing.

He found himself attentively searching the ground for a suitable place to lie with her. "I warn you," he said very low, his mouth in a lazy grin, "I'm days past the need for seduction. All I can offer you is this country setting. Do you mind?"

She smiled up at him as she put her hand in his. "As long as you hold me, my lord, and as long as the grass stains don't show."

He paused for a moment with her small hand light on his palm. "You're very remarkable," he softly said.

"Too candid for you, my lord?" she playfully inquired.

His long fingers closed around her hand in an act of possession, pure and simple, as if he would keep this spirited, plain-speaking woman who startled him. "Your candor excites me," he said. "Be warned," he murmured, drawing her to her feet. "I've been wanting you for three days' past; I won't guarantee finesse." Releasing her hand, he held his up so she could see them tremble. "Look."

"I'm shaking *inside* so violently I may savage you first, my lord," Elizabeth softly breathed, swaying toward him, her fragrance sweet in his nostrils, her face lifted for a kiss. "I've been waiting four months since I left Goldiehouse."

A spiking surge of lust ripped through his senses, gut-deep, searing, her celibacy a singular, flamboyant ornament offered to him as if it were his duty, his obligation to bring her pleasure. In a flashing moment his hands closed on her shoulders. Pulling her sharply close, his palms slid down her back—then lower, swiftly cupping her bottom. His mouth dipped to hers and he forced her mouth open, plunging his tongue deep inside.

Like a woman too long denied, Elizabeth welcomed him, pulling his head down so she could reach his mouth more easily, straining upward on tiptoes so she could feel him hard against her, tearing at the buttons on his shirt so the heat of his skin touched hers.

"Hurry, Johnnie, please . . ." she whispered.

Moonlight, Madness, & Magic

by

Suzanne Foster, Charlotte Hughes, and Olivia Rupprecht

"A beguiling mix of passion and the occult. . . . an engaging read."
—*Publishers Weekly*
"Incredibly ingenious." —*Romantic Times*

This strikingly original anthology by three of Loveswept's bestselling authors is one of the most talked about books of the year! With more than 2.5 million copies of their titles in print, these beloved authors bring their talents to a boldly imaginative collection of romantic novellas that weaves a tale of witchcraft, passion, and unconditional love set in 1785, 1872, and 1992.

Here's a look at the heart-stopping prologue . . . .

OXFORD VILLAGE, MASSACHUSETTS — 1690 Rachael Deliverance Dobbs had been beautiful once. The flaming red hair that often strayed from her morning cap and curled in wispy tendrils about her face had turned more than one shopkeeper's head. Today, however, that red hair was tangled and filthy and fell against her back and shoulders like a tattered woolen shawl.

Prison had not served her well.

"The woman hath *witchcraft* in her," an onlooker spat out as Rachael was led to the front of the meeting house, where a constable, the governor's magistrate, and several of the town selectmen waited to decide her fate. Her ankles were shackled in irons, making her progress slow and painful.

Rachael staggered, struggling to catch her balance as the magistrate peered over his spectacles at her. Clearing his throat, the magistrate began to speak, giving each word a deep and thunderous import. "Rachael Deliverance Dobbs, thou hast been accused by this court of not fearing the Almighty God as do thy good and prudent neighbors, of preternatural acts against the citizenry of Oxford, and of the heinous crime of witchcraft, for which, by the law of the colony of Massachusetts, thou deservest to die. Has thou anything to say in thy defense?"

Rachael Dobbs could barely summon the strength to deny the charges. Her accusers had kept her jailed for months, often depriving her of sleep, food, and clean water to drink. In order to secure a confession, they'd whipped her with rawhide and tortured her with hideous instruments. Though she'd been grievously injured and several of her ribs broken, she'd given them nothing.

"Nay," she said faintly, "I know not of which ye speak, m'lord. For as God is my witness, I have been wrongly accused."

A rage quickened the air, and several of the spectators rose from their seats. "Blasphemy!" someone cried. "The witch would use *His* name in vain?"

"Order!" The magistrate brought his gavel down. "Let the accused answer the charges. Goody Dobbs, it is said thou makest the devil's brew of strange plants that grow in the forest."

"I know not this devil's brew you speak of," Rachael protested. "I use the herbs for healing, just as my mother before me."

"And thou extracts a fungus from rye grass to stop birthing pains?" he queried.

"I do not believe a woman should suffer so, m'lord."

"Even though the Good Book commands it?"

"The Good Book also commands us to use the sense God gave us," she reminded him tremulously.

"I'll not tolerate this sacrilege!" The village preacher slammed his fist down on the table, inciting the onlookers into a frenzy of shouting and name-calling.

As the magistrate called for order, Rachael turned to the crowd, searching for the darkly handsome face of her betrothed, Jonathan Nightingale. She'd not been allowed visitors in jail, but surely Jonathan would be here today to speak on her behalf. With his wealth and good name, he would quickly put an end to this hysteria. That hope had kept her alive, bringing her comfort even when she'd learned her children had been placed in the care of Jonathan's housekeeper, a young woman Rachael distrusted for her deceptive ways. But that mattered little now. When Jonathaan cleared her name of these crimes, she would be united with her babes once again. How she longed to see them!

"Speak thou for me, Jonathan Nightingale?" she cried, forgetting everything but her joy at seeing him. "Thou knowest me better than anyone. Thou knowest the secrets of my heart. Tell these people I am not what they accuse me. Tell them, so that my children may be returned to me." Her voice trembled with emotion, but as Jonathan glanced up and met her eyes, she knew a moment of doubt. She didn't see the welcoming warmth she expected. Was something amiss?

At the magistrate's instruction, the bailiff called Jonathan to come forward. "State thy name for the court," the bailiff said, once he'd been sworn in.

"Jonathan Peyton Nightingale."

"Thou knowest the accused, Goody Dobbs?" the magistrate asked.

Jonathan acknowledged Rachael with a slow nod of his head. "Mistress Dobbs and I were engaged to be married before she was incarcerated," Jonathan told the magistrate. "I've assumed the care of her children these last few months. She has no family of her own."

"Hast thou anything to say in her defense?"

"She was a decent mother, to be sure. Her children be well mannered."

"And have ye reason to believe the charges against her?"

When Jonathan hesitated, the magistrate pressed him. "Prithee, do not withhold information from the court, Mr. Nightingale," he cautioned, "lest thee find thyself in the same dire predicament as the accused. Conspiring to protect a witch is a lawful test of guilt."

Startled, Jonathan could only stare at the stern-faced tribunal before him. It had never occured to him that his association with Rachael could put him in a hangman's noose as well. He had been searching his soul since she'd been jailed, wondering how much he was morally bound to reveal at this trial. Now he saw little choice but to unburden himself.

"After she was taken, I found this among her things," he said, pulling an object from his coat pocket and unwrapping it. He avoided looking at Rachael, anticipating the stricken expression he would surely see in her eyes. "It's an image made of horsehair. A woman's image. There be a pin stuck through it."

The crowd gasped as Jonathan held up the effigy. A woman screamed, and even the magistrate drew back in horror.

Rachael sat in stunned disbelief. An icy fist closed around her heart. How could Jonathan have done such a thing? Did he not realize he'd signed her death warrant? Dear merciful God, if they found her guilty, she would never see her children again!

" 'Twas mere folly that I fashioned the image, m'lord," she told the magistrate. "I suspected my betrothed of dallying with his housekeeper. I fear my temper bested me."

"And was it folly when thou gavest Goodwife Brown's child the evil eye and caused her to languish with the fever?" the magistrate probed.

" 'Twas coincidence, m'lord," she said, imploring him to believe her. "The child was ill when I arrived at Goody Brown's house. I merely tried to help her." Rachael could see the magistrate's skepticism, and she whirled to Jonathan in desperation. "How canst thou doubt me, Jonathan?" she asked.

He hung his head. He was torn with regret, even shame. He loved Rachael, but God help him, he had no wish to die beside her. One had only to utter the word *witch* these days to end up on the gallows. Not that Rachael hadn't given all of them cause to suspect her. When he'd found the effigy, he'd told himself she must have been maddened by jealousy. But truly he didn't understand her anymore. She'd stopped going to Sunday services and more than once had induced him to lie abed with her on a Sabbath morn. "Methinks thou hast bewitched me as well, Rachael," he replied.

Another gasp from the crowd.

"Hanging is too good for her!" a woman shouted.

"Burn her!" another cried from the front row. "Before she bewitches us all."

Rachael bent her head in despair, all hope draining from her. Her own betrothed had forsaken her, and his condemnation meant certain death. There was no one who could save her now. And yet, in the depths of her desolation, a spark of rage kindled.

"So be it," she said, seized by a black hysteria. She was beyond caring now, beyond the crowd's censure or their grace. No one could take anything more from her than had already been taken. Jonathan's engagement gift to her, a golden locket, hung at her neck. She ripped it free and flung it at him.

"Thou shall have thy desire, Jonathan Nightingale," she cried. "And pay for it dearly. Since thou hast consigned me to the gallows and stolen my children from me, I shall put a blood curse on thee and thine."

The magistrate pounded his gavel against the table, ordering the spectators to silence. "Mistress Dobbs!" he warned, his voice harsh, "I fear thou hast just sealed thy fate."

But Rachael would not be deterred. Her heart was aflame with the fury of a woman betrayed. "Hear me good, Jonathan," she said, oblivious of the magistrate, of everyone but the man she'd once loved with all her being. "Thou hast damned my soul to hell, but I'll not burn there alone. I curse the Nightingale seed to a fate worse than the flames of Hades. Your progeny shall be as the living dead, denied the rest of the grave."

Her voice dropped to a terrifying hush as she began to intone the curse. "The third son of every third son shall walk the earth as a creature of the night, trapped in shadows, no two creatures alike. Stripped of humanity, he will howl in concert with demons, never to die, always to wander in agony, until a woman entraps his heart and soul as thee did mine—"

"My God, she is truly the devil's mistress!" the preacher gasped. A cry rose from the crowd, and several of them surged forward, trying to stop her. Guards rushed to block them.

"Listen to me, Jonathan!" Rachael cried over the din. "I've not finished with thee yet. If that woman should find a way to set the creature free, it will be at great and terrible cost. A sacrifice no mortal woman would ever be willing to make—"

She hesitated, her chin beginning to tremble as hot tears pooled in her eyes. Glistening, they slid down her cheeks, burning her tender flesh before they dropped to the wooden floor. But as they hit the planks, something astonishing happened. Even

Rachael in her grief was amazed. The teardrops hardened before everyone's eyes into precious gems. Flashing in the sunlight was a dazzling blue-white diamond, a blood-red ruby, and a brilliant green emerald.

The crowd was stunned to silence.

Rachael glanced up, aware of Jonathan's fear, of everyone's astonishment. Their gaping stares brought her a fleeting sense of triumph. Her curse had been heard.

"Rachael Dobbs, confess thy sins before this court and thy Creator!" the magistrate bellowed.

But it was too late for confessions. The doors to the courtroom burst open, and a pack of men streamed in with blazing pine torches. "Goody Brown's child is dead of the fits," they shouted. "The witch must burn!"

The guards couldn't hold back the vigilantes, and Rachael closed her eyes as the pack of men engulfed her. She said a silent good-bye to her children as she was gripped by bruising hands and lifted off the ground. She could feel herself being torn nearly apart as they dragged her from the meeting room, but she did not cry out. She felt no physical pain. She had just made a pact with the forces of darkness, and she could no longer feel anything except the white-hot inferno of the funeral pyre that would soon release her to her everlasting vigil.

She welcomed it, just as she welcomed the sweet justice that would one day be hers. She would not die in vain. Her curse had been heard.

"Fayrene Preston has an uncanny ability
to create intense atmosphere that
is truly superb."
—*Romantic Times*

Satin and Steele
by
Fayrene Preston

SATIN AND STEELE *is a classic favorite of fans of
Fayrene Preston. Originally published under the pseud-
onym Jaelyn Conlee, this novel was the talented Ms.
Preston's first ever published novel. We are thrilled to
offer you the opportunity to read this long-unavailable
book in its new Bantam edition.*

Skye Anderson knew the joy and wonder of love—as
well as the pain of its tragic loss. She'd carved a new
life for herself at Dallas' Hayes Corporation, finding
security in a cocoon of hard-working days and lonely
nights. Then her company is taken over by the leg-
endary corporate raider James Steele and once again
Skye must face the possibility of losing everything
she cares about. When Steele enlists her aid in
organizing the new company, she is determined to
prove herself worthy of the challenge. But as they
work together side by side, Skye can't deny that
she feels more than a professional interest in her

new boss—and that the feeling is mutual. Soon she would have to decide whether to let go of her desire for Steele once and for all—or risk everything for a second chance at love.

OFFICIAL RULES

To enter the sweepstakes below carefully follow all instructions found elsewhere in this offer.

The **Winners Classic** will award prizes with the following approximate maximum values: 1 Grand Prize: $26,500 (or $25,000 cash alternate); 1 First Prize: $3,000; 5 Second Prizes: $400 each; 35 Third Prizes: $100 each; 1,000 Fourth Prizes: $7.50 each. Total maximum retail value of Winners Classic Sweepstakes is $42,500. Some presentations of this sweepstakes may contain individual entry numbers corresponding to one or more of the aforementioned prize levels. To determine the Winners, individual entry numbers will first be compared with the winning numbers preselected by computer. For winning numbers not returned, prizes will be awarded in random drawings from among all eligible entries received. Prize choices may be offered at various levels. If a winner chooses an automobile prize, all license and registration fees, taxes, destination charges and, other expenses not offered herein are the responsibility of the winner. If a winner chooses a trip, travel must be complete within one year from the time the prize is awarded. Minors must be accompanied by an adult. Travel companion(s) must also sign release of liability. Trips are subject to space and departure availability. Certain black-out dates may apply.

The following applies to the sweepstakes named above:

No purchase necessary. You can also enter the sweepstakes by sending your name and address to: P.O. Box 508, Gibbstown, N.J. 08027. Mail each entry separately. Sweepstakes begins 6/1/93. Entries must be received by 12/30/94. Not responsible for lost, late, damaged, misdirected, illegible or postage due mail. Mechanically reproduced entries are not eligible. All entries become property of the sponsor and will not be returned.

Prize Selection/Validations: Selection of winners will be conducted no later than 5:00 PM on January 28, 1995, by an independent judging organization whose decisions are final. Random drawings will be held at 1211 Avenue of the Americas, New York, N.Y. 10036. Entrants need not be present to win. Odds of winning are determined by total number of entries received. Circulation of this sweepstakes is estimated not to exceed 200 million. All prizes are guaranteed to be awarded and delivered to winners. Winners will be notified by mail and may be required to complete an affidavit of eligibility and release of liability which must be returned within 14 days of date on notification or alternate winners will be selected in a random drawing. Any prize notification letter or any prize returned to a participating sponsor, Bantam Doubleday Dell Publishing Group, Inc., its participating divisions or subsidiaries, or the independent judging organization as undeliverable will be awarded to an alternate winner. Prizes are not transferable. No substitution for prizes except as offered or as may be necessary due to unavailability, in which case a prize of equal or greater value will be awarded. Prizes will be awarded approximately 90 days after the drawing. All taxes are the sole responsibility of the winners. Entry constitutes permission (except where prohibited by law) to use winners' names, hometowns, and likenesses for publicity purposes without further or other compensation. Prizes won by minors will be awarded in the name of parent or legal guardian.

Participation: Sweepstakes open to residents of the United States and Canada, except for the province of Quebec. Sweepstakes sponsored by Bantam Doubleday Dell Publishing Group, Inc., (BDD), 1540 Broadway, New York, NY 10036. Versions of this sweepstakes with different graphics and prize choices will be offered in conjunction with various solicitations or promotions by different subsidiaries and divisions of BDD. Where applicable, winners will have their choice of any prize offered at level won. Employees of BDD, its divisions, subsidiaries, advertising agencies, independent judging organization, and their immediate family members are not eligible.

Canadian residents, in order to win, must first correctly answer a time limited arithmetical skill testing question. Void in Puerto Rico, Quebec and wherever prohibited or restricted by law. Subject to all federal, state, local and provincial laws and regulations. For a list of major prize winners (available after 1/29/95): send a self-addressed, stamped envelope separate from your entry to: Sweepstakes Winners, P.O. Box 517, Gibbstown, NJ 08027. Requests must be received by 12/30/94. DO NOT SEND ANY OTHER CORRESPONDENCE TO THIS P.O. BOX.

Don't miss these fabulous Bantam women's fiction titles

now on sale

• OUTLAW
by Susan Johnson, author of SINFUL & FORBIDDEN

From the supremely talented mistress of erotic historical romance comes a sizzling love story of a fierce Scottish border lord who abducts his sworn enemy, a beautiful English woman — only to find himself a captive of her love.

____29955-7 $5.50/6.50 in Canada

• MOONLIGHT, MADNESS, AND MAGIC
by Suzanne Forster, Charlotte Hughes, and Olivia Rupprecht

Three romantic supernatural novellas set in 1785, 1872, and 1992. "Incredibly ingenious." — Romantic Times
"Something for everyone." — Gothic Journal
"An engaging read." — Publishers Weekly
"Exemplary." — Rendezvous   ____56052-2 $5.50/6.50 in Canada

• SATIN AND STEELE
by Fayrene Preston, co-author of THE DELANEY CHRISTMAS CAROL

Fayrene Preston's classic tale of a woman who thought she could never love again, and a man who thought love had passed him by.   ____56457-9 $4.50/5.50 in Canada

**Ask for these books at your local bookstore
or use this page to order.**

❏ Please send me the books I have checked above. I am enclosing $ _____ (add $2.50 to cover postage and handling). Send check or money order, no cash or C. O. D.'s please.

Name _____

Address _____

City/ State/ Zip _____

Send order to: Bantam Books, Dept. FN120, 2451 S. Wolf Rd., Des Plaines, IL 60018
Allow four to six weeks for delivery.
Prices and availability subject to change without notice.

FN120 11/93

Don't miss these fabulous Bantam women's fiction titles

on sale in November

• NOTORIOUS
by Patricia Potter, author of *RENEGADE*

Long ago, Catalina Hilliard had vowed never to give away her heart, but she hadn't counted on the spark of desire that flared between her and her business rival, Marsh Canton. Now that desire is about to spin Cat's carefully orchestrated life out of control.

_____56225-8 $5.50/6.50 in Canada

• PRINCESS OF THIEVES
by Katherine O'Neal, author of *THE LAST HIGHWAYMAN*

Mace Blackwood was a daring rogue—the greatest con artist in the world. Saranda Sherwin was a master thief who used her wits and wiles to make tough men weak. And when Saranda's latest charade leads to tragedy and sends her fleeing for her life, Mace is compelled to follow, no matter what the cost.

_____56066-2 $5.50/$6.50 in Canada

• CAPTURE THE NIGHT
by Geralyn Dawson

In this "Once Upon a Time" Romance with "Beauty and the Beast" at its heart, Geralyn Dawson weaves the love story of a runaway beauty, the Texan who rescues her, and their precious stolen "Rose."

_____56176-6 $4.99/5.99 in Canada